cathy cassidy

Driftwood

PUFFIN

PUFFIN BOOKS

Published by the Penguin Group
Penguin Books Ltd, 80 Strand, London WC2R ORL, England
Penguin Group (USA) Inc., 375 Hudson Street, New York, New York 10014, USA
Penguin Group (Canada), 90 Eglinton Avenue East, Suite 700, Toronto, Ontario, Canada M4P 2Y3
(a division of Pearson Penguin Canada Inc.)
Penguin Ireland, 25 St Stephen's Green, Dublin 2, Ireland (a division of Penguin Books Ltd)
Penguin Group (Australia), 250 Camberwell Road, Camberwell, Victoria 3124, Australia
(a division of Pearson Australia Group Pty Ltd)
Penguin Books India Pvt Ltd, 11 Community Centre, Panchsheel Park, New Delhi – 110 017, India
Penguin Group (NZ), 67 Apollo Drive, Rosedale, North Shore 0632, New Zealand
(a division of Pearson New Zealand Ltd)
Penguin Books (South Africa) (Pty) Ltd, 24 Sturdee Avenue, Rosebank,
Johannesburg 2196, South Africa

Penguin Books Ltd, Registered Offices: 80 Strand, London WC2R ORL, England

puffinbooks.com

First published 2005
This edition produced for The Book People Ltd, Hall Wood Avenue,
Haydock, St Helens WA11 9UL
1

Set in 13/16.5 pt Monotype Baskerville
by Palimpsest Book Production Limited, Grangemouth, Stirlingshire
Made and printed in England by Clays Ltd, St Ives plc

British Library Cataloguing in Publication Data
A CIP catalogue record for this book is available from the British Library

ISBN: 978-1-856-13246-6

www.greenpenguin.co.uk

Hiya!

A little while ago, I was at a craft fair and fell in love with a cool mirror decorated with pale, twisty bits of driftwood. I kept wondering about what it'd be like to live by the sea and make fab things. Who would do that kind of thing? What kind of house would they have?

Before long, I had created a whole bunch of characters, and those characters had a story to tell. *Driftwood* is a story about friendship, fitting in and falling in love, all mixed in with a little bit of magic and a trio of crazy kittens (based on my three thuggish mogs!). It's for everyone out there who feels different from the crowd, who doesn't fit in - and anyone who has ever been bullied.

I got to mooch around a lot of windswept beaches while researching the book, and I collected vast piles of driftwood along the way! I loved writing about Joey, Hannah, Kit and Paul - I hope you'll love reading about them too.

Best wishes,

Cathy Cassidy

xxxx ✾

cathycassidy.com

Books by Cathy Cassidy

DIZZY
DRIFTWOOD
INDIGO BLUE
SCARLETT
SUNDAE GIRL
LUCKY STAR

Thanks!

As ever, to Liam and Calum for their love, hugs and endless support, and Caitlin, who gave me the idea for Joey in the book! Thanks also to Mum, Dad, Andy, Lori, Joan and my whole fab family. Special thanks to my first readers, Catriona, Fiona and Mary-Jane, and also Helen, Sheena, Zarah and all my lovely friends – whether it's swimming, climbing hills, eating cake or just talking, you're always there for me.

Thanks to Paul for knitting me such a cool website, and Martyn for doing the adding-up bits. Thanks to Darley and his angels, Julia, Lucy and all at the agency, and to Rebecca, Francesca, Adele, Tania, Shannon, Kirsten, Jo and all at Puffin HQ for believing in me.

To the kids who email the website or write to me, a huge thank you – your enthusiasm and encouragement is the best. Last, but not least, thanks to the fab and talented pupils at Kells, Carsphairn, Springholm, St Peters, Crossmichael and Gelston schools for your knack of putting a smile on my face every time I'm teaching. I'm gonna miss you! (Sniff!)

CHAPTER 1

My best friend, Joey Donovan, is weird. She is clever, she is kind, she is seriously cool, but still, she's weird, in a take-it-or-leave-it kind of way.

She always has been, ever since she marched into my classroom seven years ago, wearing pink wellies, reindeer antlers and a don't-mess-with-me look in her big blue eyes. She pitched up in Kirklaggan like a small tornado, and she's been like that ever since.

It's Monday morning, and Joey stomps down the aisle of the school bus, a vision in freckles and black lipstick.

She's wearing a grey school skirt with the hem chopped off so it's all frayed and ratty, and long stripy socks that reach up over her skinny knees.

One sock is black and white, the other black and red. On her feet are clumpy black biker boots with shiny silver buckles, and her jacket is a huge, drooping school blazer like something your great-grandad might have worn in 1947. Where the school badge once was, she has stitched on a Good Charlotte patch, slightly squint.

She is on a one-woman mission to overthrow school uniform, or redesign it as her own version of punk/goth/scarecrow chic. She is twelve years old.

'Like the socks,' my brother, Kit, calls down from the back seat of the bus. A few kids snigger, and Joey sticks her tongue out at him, but hey, my brother probably *does* like the socks. He is thirteen years old and lately I have seen a moonstruck, fuzzy expression seep over his face whenever Joey is around.

I haven't mentioned this to Joey yet. I don't want to scare her.

She slides into the seat beside me. Her hair, ash blonde with random stripes of pink and green, is bundled into two stubby plaits that stick out alarmingly above her collar.

'Major news!' she says, eyes sparkling with excitement. 'I mean, seriously major, Hannah! You will never *guess* what happened yesterday!'

Yesterday, Joey was meant to come round to my

place to hang out, use my PC for her English homework and get her usual fix of *The Simpsons*. Jed and Eva don't have a computer or a telly in their house, and Joey gets withdrawal symptoms sometimes. At the last minute, she rang to cancel.

I didn't mind too much, but Kit was crushed, all dressed up in his best jeans and hoodie, hair gelled into hedgehog spikes and trailing a cloud of toxic aftershave. He's got it bad.

'So,' I say now, tugging at Joey's plait, 'what was it all about? Tell!'

She settles into her seat, breaking a stick of gum in half so we can share. 'Guess what? Jed and Eva are only going to foster a new kid! After all this time!'

Joey and her little brother, Mikey, started out being fostered, but their family, Jed and Eva, got the legal bits sorted and adopted them for keeps a few years back. If you saw the Donovan family all together you'd never guess they weren't related. They are a perfect fit – the whole bunch of them are seriously flaky.

'No way!' I grin. 'A new kid? Is that good or bad?'

'Oh, good, definitely,' Joey laughs. 'Paul, his name is. Paul Slater. The social workers said he's from a troubled background, whatever that is, but they reckon he'll settle in great with Jed and Eva.

They brought him down from Glasgow yesterday. Cool or what?'

'Cool. How old is he? Will he be a friend for Mikey?'

'Nah,' Joey says. 'Paul's older than us – thirteen. He'll be in S2. Maybe Kit can look out for him?'

My brother, Kit, is a pain in the bum, but he's funny and streetwise and popular with the other kids. And, in spite of the teasing, he'd do anything for Joey.

'Why don't you ask him?' I suggest. 'I think he'd do it.'

'I will. Paul's starting school today, but Eva drove him in early to get the paperwork done, and to talk to Mr McKenzie and the guidance teachers and everyone.'

The bus lurches to a halt and a sea of rackety teenagers rolls down the aisle. Joey and I take our time. It's January. It's only just light out there, and definitely sub-zero, so what's the hurry? When Joey stands up, my brother, Kit, just happens to be in the aisle behind her.

'Fancy seeing you girls,' he says carelessly, as if he hasn't spent a whole week planning this exact moment. 'After you, Josephine.'

'Why, thank you, Christopher,' Joey says sweetly.

Kit moves smoothly along behind her, bashing me in the arm with his rucksack, so I know this sudden attack of good manners doesn't extend to me.

Joey is telling Kit about the new foster-kid, and by the time we spill out, shivering, on to the frosty pavements, she's got him to promise he'll keep an eye on Paul Slater.

'Just until he finds his feet, y'know,' Joey is saying. 'He's quite shy, I think, but he *is* from Glasgow. He must have a bit of street sense somewhere.'

'Leave it to me,' Kit replies. 'I'll look after him.'

'Oh, Kit, *thanks*,' Joey says, fluttering her eyelashes and laying it on thick. 'I knew I could count on you.'

By the time she turns away from him, my brother is bright pink and grinning like a madman. No change there, then.

We link arms and mooch up towards the school gates, giggling.

'Your brother *blushed*,' Joey tells me, although just about everyone south of Aberdeen must have spotted the beacon that is Kit's face. 'D'you think he likes me?'

'Just a bit.'

'Whoa.' Joey laughs. 'Don't know if I can handle that.'

'Don't know if *I* can!'

Then we spot Mr McKenzie, the Head, patrolling the school gates. We stop dead in our tracks. Mr

McKenzie and Joey Donovan do not see eye to eye. His aim in life is to stamp out all signs of rebellion, disorder and individuality. School uniform offences are punishable by death, or week-long detentions, anyhow. Joey does not stand a chance.

'We'll sneak in through the staff car park,' I decide, dragging Joey along the pavement, away from the main gates.

Joey looks glum, because she enjoys arguing about uniform with Mr McKenzie. Since she started at Kirklaggan High School last August, he's had to write two new clauses into the school uniform list. The first outlaws black PVC miniskirts, the second declares that dog collars and studded wristbands may not be worn on school premises.

'Freak,' spits out an S3 lad as we dodge past him.

'Loser,' Joey responds automatically.

When I look over my shoulder, I can see Kit giving the S3 kid a row for picking on Joey, and I have to smile.

We sneak through the teachers' car park and skirt round the back of the dinner halls. A heady aroma of boiled cabbage and custard assaults us from the kitchens, even though it's barely ten to nine.

'What's that noise?' Joey demands suddenly, frowning.

'Can't hear anything. C'mon, Joey, we can't be late.'

Joey is standing still, her face anxious, eyes scanning the kitchen yard with its skip full of cardboard, the piles of plastic crates and the trio of dustbins huddled together near the wall.

'I heard something,' she insists.

'I didn't,' I huff. It's so cold the words seem to gather in the air before me; a small white cloud, like dragon's breath. 'Joey, it's freezing. Can we just go now?'

She shakes her head, putting a finger to her lips. Exasperated, I shiver inside my duffel coat.

'What kind of a noise?' I ask. In the stillness I can hear the sound of kids shouting in the distance, and someone scraping a pan inside the kitchen. Behind us, Miss Quinn's clapped-out VW Beetle wheezes across the car park and shudders to a halt.

'Shhh.'

The school bell clatters out then, and Miss Quinn rushes past us, pink scarf flapping, on her way to the art block. 'Hurry up, girls,' she grins. 'You'll be late. Later than me, even!' She disappears round the corner, but Joey still won't budge.

And then I hear it: a thin, mewling cry that's coming from the dustbins.

Joey's there in a flash, tipping up the lids, rooting through the rubbish. Scrunched-up kitchen roll and long strips of cellophane flutter down on to the concrete.

'Hannah,' she breathes. 'Look, Hannah, just *look* what I've found.'

Together we peer inside the third bin. They're in among the vegetable peelings and the cold baked beans, curled in a squashed-up cardboard box, chucked out in the freezing cold January morning like so much rubbish.

Three tiny, shivering, blue-eyed kittens.

CHAPTER 2

Joey has a kitten in each pocket of her outsize school blazer, and I cradle a wriggling scrap of tortoiseshell fur inside my woolly hat.

'Oh, Hannah, who would do such a thing?' Joey demands, outraged. 'They could have been there all night, for all we know. It's barbaric!'

'They could have died,' I whisper, gazing down at the tiny kitten in my hands. 'They still could, Joey. We have to get them warm and safe and fed. Fast!'

'What shall we do?'

I chew my lip. 'They need food *now*. We need somewhere safe, somewhere warm. We need someone who'll understand.'

'Miss Quinn,' we say together.

If any teacher in the school will help, it has to be Miss Quinn. She's cool and kind and she doesn't tell Joey off for wearing funny clothes or having stripy hair. She lets us listen to music in class and gives us sweets at the end of term.

The art room is where we hang out on rainy days, along with a whole raft of other kids who take refuge there, finishing off work or doing extra stuff of their own. Miss Quinn doesn't mind as long as we're working, as long as it's art. She just smiles and nibbles ginger biscuits, and sips milky coffee that she makes with a plug-in kettle she keeps in the stock cupboard. She's OK, Miss Quinn. You know she's on your side.

The bell that signals the end of registration has just rung, so we leg it round to the front of the school. Joey and I melt into the crowds and pass unnoticed. Joey keeps her hands in her pockets, and I hide the hat under my duffel coat.

Outside the first-floor art room, I take a deep breath, rap on the door and go in.

Amazingly, Miss Quinn has a free lesson. She is alone in an empty classroom, listening to a classical music CD, spreading out screen-prints for a class discussion after break. I spot Kit's design – a skateboarder silhouetted against a rainbow background – so I know that the next class is his.

'Girls?' Miss Quinn looks up, confused. 'I don't

see your class until Friday afternoon, do I? Is there a problem?'

'Kind of,' Joey begins, scooping the kittens out of her pockets and on to the tabletop, where they stand on wobbly legs.

'You have to help us, Miss,' I add, bringing out the fur-filled hat from under my coat. The littlest kitten scratches and mews and blinks a few times under the electric lights.

'Joey, Hannah!' Miss Quinn gasps. 'Where on earth did you find them? They're only a few weeks old. They shouldn't even be away from their mother!'

'They've been abandoned,' I whisper. 'They were in the bins round the back of the kitchens, just stuffed in with all the rubbish. They're cold and starving, but we have to save them, Miss. Will you help? Please?'

She looks at us, stricken. 'Of course I'll help,' she says. 'The stock cupboard's the warmest place; the pipes for the central heating run right through it. We'll put them in there.'

Miss Quinn empties a cardboard box full of SI clay tiles and lines it with her own pink mohair scarf. We lift the kittens in, one by one, and wedge the box beneath the warm pipes in the stockroom, in between crates of paint and baskets of torn tissue paper. Miss Quinn pours milk into a jam jar, and puts the kettle on to boil while she fishes around in a drawer for the ink-droppers we used last term to drip marbling ink on to water as part of our print project. When the kettle's hot, she stirs a little water into the cold milk and fills an ink-dropper.

'I don't know if this is the right thing,' Miss Quinn admits. 'I don't know if they'll take it. But it's milk, and it's warm. We can try.'

The liveliest kitten, tabby with white paws, takes the dropper in its mouth. Miss Quinn squeezes the top and a bubble of milk appears. The other two kittens start yowling. Joey and I fill an ink-dropper each.

'We'll need to ring the animal shelter,' Miss Quinn says. 'They'll know what to do, how to look after them. They'll be able to find homes for these little guys once they're old enough.'

I look down at the scrap of tortoiseshell fur, button eyes gazing at me full of trust. My heart plummets.

'No way,' Joey says firmly. 'They're not going to any old animal shelter. These kittens have a home – with me. Jed and Eva will be fine with it, and Hannah can have the tortoiseshell one as soon as it's old enough to be separated.'

'Oh, yes, Miss,' I cry. 'Please? We can manage, really we can.'

Miss Quinn looks doubtful.

'These kittens can't be more than three or four weeks old. They need to be fed every few hours, through the night as well as the daytime.'

'We can do it,' I insist.

'We found them, Miss,' Joey points out. 'We saved them. Please don't make us give them away.'

'They're crawling with fleas,' Miss Quinn says, wrinkling up her nose as the trio start scratching. 'Poor little things. The little tortoiseshell one's got scabs in its fur too. They'll need to see a vet.'

'We can sort that,' Joey promises. 'Please?'

'I must be crazy,' Miss Quinn says. 'OK, give it a go. You can stay with them till the end of break – I'll write you a couple of late passes so you don't get into trouble. If you come in again at lunchtime to feed them, they might just sleep all afternoon . . .'

Joey grins. 'Thanks, Miss – you're the coolest!'

'Keep this quiet, you two,' Miss Quinn warns. 'I don't want half the school trooping in to admire these little wretches.'

'No problem,' Joey promises. 'Our lips are sealed.'

Just as the kittens finish feeding and settle down to sleep, there's a sharp rap on the classroom door.

'Miss Quinn?' a stern voice calls. 'Are you there?'

'It's McKenzie!' Joey yelps. '*Mr* McKenzie, I mean.'

'Stay here,' Miss Quinn whispers. 'And keep quiet.'

She swoops out of the stock cupboard, switching off the light and letting the door swing shut behind her. Joey and I crouch beside the kittens, trying to stay still and silent.

'Ah, Miss Quinn, good, good,' Mr McKenzie's voice booms out. The classical music CD reaches an especially loud and rumbly bit, then gets cut off rudely in midstream.

'We don't need that, do we?' Mr McKenzie barks. 'Now, Miss Quinn, we have a new pupil starting school today, and I'm told that art is his best subject. Isn't that right, Paul?'

There's a grunt from outside the stockroom door, and Joey pinches my arm, hard. 'It's him!' she hisses. 'The new foster-kid, Paul!'

'Miss Quinn will be taking you for art, and your first lesson is . . . ah, after break, in fact,' Mr McKenzie rumbles on. 'Miss Quinn is an excellent teacher – we're very proud of our art department here at Kirklaggan.'

'I think you also teach my daughter, Joey Donovan?' a soft, familiar voice asks. Eva.

'That's right,' Miss Quinn says.

'Ah, yes, *Josephine*,' Mr McKenzie cuts in. 'A very bright girl, but there are some uniform issues I should like to discuss with you, Mrs Donovan. And *attitude* issues . . .'

Joey blows a loud raspberry, which wakes the kittens up. They start mewling loudly, perhaps hoping for more milk.

'What's that noise?' Mr McKenzie demands. 'Is it coming from the stock cupboard?'

'That'll be the central-heating pipes again,' Miss Quinn says smoothly. 'They've been making some dreadful noises lately.'

'Oh? I'll ask the janitor to look at them for you,' Mr McKenzie tells her. 'Well, that just about finishes the guided tour. Your class are at games right now, Paul, and the lesson is nearly over, so perhaps you'd better join them after break for art instead? You can stay here if you like, and show those sketchbooks to Miss Quinn.'

'OK,' a quiet voice says.

The art-room door creaks open, and we hear Mr McKenzie usher Eva out of the room, explaining that stripy socks and matching hair are not really part of the uniform code.

'Phew,' Joey breathes. 'I thought he'd catch us for sure. We'd have been in serious trouble!'

'And Miss Quinn too, for hiding us,' I point out. 'Cut the raspberries next time!'

We peer round the door. Miss Quinn is writing out a couple of late passes for us, magic slips of paper that will allow us to join our next class unchallenged. Paul Slater, the new boy, is on the other side of the classroom, looking out of the window. I can only see the back of him: tall and slim and somehow graceful-looking.

'So, Paul,' Miss Quinn calls over. 'Art is your favourite subject, is it? What do you like best? We do clay work, textiles, graphics, 3-D, art history and, of course, drawing and painting.'

'I like comic-book art,' the boy says. His voice is surprisingly soft and gentle.

'Do you? Excellent!' Miss Quinn declares. 'Shall I have a look at those sketchbooks, then?'

We edge up behind her as she leafs through three dog-eared books of cartoon sketches. The drawings are clean, clear, beautifully drawn, some in pencil, some in black ink, some in felt pen. They are streets ahead of anything I could do.

'Hey, Paul, these are cool,' Joey says. 'Really.'

The boy turns, and I can see he has floppy, mid-brown hair that falls in messy waves round his face. His skin is pale and his eyes are a startling sea green.

'Joey,' he says, smiling slightly. 'Hi. What are you doing here?'

'Ah, wouldn't you like to know,' Joey grins. 'Can we tell him, Miss? Reckon he can keep a secret?'

'Oh, I should think so.'

'This is my best mate, Hannah Murray,' Joey says with a sweep of her arm. 'She lives just down the road from us. And you will never guess what we found this morning . . .'

There's another peal of mewling from the stock cupboard, and I sprint in to check the kittens are OK. I decide they're still hungry, and fill another ink-dropper with milk.

'See?' Joey is saying. 'In the box, down there. Aren't they gorgeous? Aren't they cute? We found them in a bin behind the school kitchens, abandoned.'

Paul Slater kneels down and puts his hand out to stroke the kittens. His fingers are long and skinny, with raggedy nails that look like they've been chewed. The kittens wriggle and squirm beneath his touch, getting playful and cheeky.

'Used to have a cat, back home,' he says. 'Long time ago.'

He looks up at me through a tangle of toffee-coloured hair. I look at his sea-green eyes, then back down at the mewling tortoiseshell kitten.

Is it possible to fall in love twice in one morning?

I think maybe it is.

CHAPTER 3

When the last bell goes, Joey and I sprint for the art room. Miss Quinn has the cardboard box ready, with air holes poked through all round the top and flaps folded shut.

'Are you sure about this?' she asks us. 'We could still call the animal shelter . . .'

'There's no need,' Joey says firmly. 'Hannah and I can do this, I promise.'

Miss Quinn sighs. 'Take the ink-droppers, then. And remember, you need to buy baby milk – the powdered, formula stuff – and get them to a vet for a check-up. Take care.'

'We will, Miss,' I grin. 'And thank you!'

We clatter down the stairs and out into the courtyard, walking briskly towards the main gates where the school buses are lined up. We get ambushed just outside the science block.

'Josephine Donovan,' Mr McKenzie says smugly. 'I've been hoping to catch up with you. Lipstick – off.'

He wafts a tissue in front of her. Joey takes it and makes black kiss-prints all over it.

'Tomorrow, Miss Donovan, we'll have socks that match, and no stripes.'

'Are stripes against the rules?' Joey asks, wide-eyed and innocent. 'I don't remember it saying that in the school uniform leaflet . . .'

'Well, it does,' Mr McKenzie snaps. 'At least, it will do soon. Plain socks. White, preferably. And this – this – *blazer*. It looks like you got it from a jumble sale.'

'I did, sir,' Joey chirps brightly. 'And blazers are definitely in the uniform leaflet. *Black blazer, with badge*, it says.'

'This is *not* the badge,' McKenzie growls, fingering the Good Charlotte patch. 'The whole thing is threadbare, and far too big for you. It's disgusting.'

'But, Mr McKenzie, I bought it specially!'

'Sir, we need to go,' I butt in, tugging gently at Joey's sleeve. 'Our bus will be leaving.'

Mr McKenzie shoots me a defeated look.

'Plain, matching socks tomorrow,' he warns. 'No

lipstick. And do something about that blazer. And the hair!'

We break into a run, and the kittens, slithering about in the box, start wailing loudly.

'Hannah Murray!' Mr McKenzie booms out behind us. 'What have you got in that box?'

'Did you hear something?' Joey asks me, grabbing the box and taking the lead.

'Nah,' I puff. 'Not a thing.'

We jump on to the bus just as the doors are closing, find the last empty seat and stash the kitten box out of sight on the floor. The school bus is so noisy, nobody can hear their mewling. They've survived a night in the dustbins and a stay in the art-room stock cupboard, and they'll survive the racket of unruly schoolkids and the roar of the engine too. I hope.

By the time we're out on the coast road, the bus is quieter – most of the kids have got off. Paul Slater moves up the bus and flops down in the seat opposite.

'Kittens OK?' he asks, his green eyes solemn.

I fish out the box, peer in through the lid. 'They're fine.'

'Sure they are,' Joey says with conviction. 'We fed them again at lunchtime, and Miss Quinn gave them some more just before the bell. Just wait till Jed and Eva see them!'

'They won't mind?' Paul asks.

'No way. They'll love it,' Joey assures him. 'You're coming too, aren't you, Hannah? Stay for tea, help the kittens settle in. Jed can drop you back.'

'Sure. Cool.'

I wouldn't miss out on the kittens' first evening at Beachcomber Cottage for anything. The fact that Paul Slater will be there too is just an added bonus.

Joey takes out a mirror and starts to reapply black lippy, a little shakily, and my brother, Kit, zigzags down the aisle and into the seat in front. He turns round to watch Joey, enjoying the view.

'Kit, I'm going over to Joey's for tea,' I tell him. 'Let Mum and Dad know, OK?'

'S'pose,' Kit shrugs. 'What's in the box?'

'Nothing!' the three of us chorus, a bit too quickly.

'Kind of a noisy nothing,' Kit says as a frenzy of squeaking and scratching starts up inside the box. 'Is it hamsters?'

'No,' Joey grins. 'You'll never guess . . .'

'He won't have to, Joey.' I sigh heavily. 'You're going to tell him, aren't you?'

'We can trust him, can't we?' she appeals. 'He's your brother!'

'Exactly.'

'Just tell,' Kit grins. 'What is it? A baby crocodile? A bunch of stolen mice from the science lab?'

Joey opens the lid a crack to show him.

'Sheesh kebab!' he says. 'Kittens! Where d'you get them? What're you gonna do with them?'

Joey gets up as the bus shudders to a halt. 'We're keeping them,' she says. 'I'm taking them back to Beachcomber Cottage. Come and see. Stay and eat if you like. Right, Paul?'

'Whatever,' Paul shrugs.

'Might just do that,' Kit says, grinning. 'Why not?'

I can think of plenty of reasons why not, but I can't do a thing about it. We pile off on to the pavement, Kit in tow. In the corner shop, we buy baby-milk powder, plus a quarter of lemon-sherbet sweets to bribe Jed and Eva.

'Not that they'll *need* bribing,' Joey says confidently. 'The Donovan family specialize in rescuing things. Driftwood from the beach, rubbish from skips, assorted waifs and strays . . .'

Paul Slater frowns and hides behind his hair.

'She doesn't mean it,' I say, falling into step beside him. 'She's just being funny. She and Mikey were waifs and strays once too.'

'I don't need to be rescued,' Paul says roughly. 'This is only a temporary placement. They always are. I've stayed in three or four different children's homes too.'

I try to think of a way of asking how that feels,

but I can't get the words out. I think I'm scared of what he'll say. When someone says *troubled background*, it conjures up an image of shaven heads, ciggies and biro-pen tattoos that say *kill*. Paul's troubled background looks like a different kind.

I'm out of my depth.

'How was school?' I drop the question into the silence. 'Think you'll settle in?'

Paul Slater shrugs. 'It's OK, I guess. Kit was friendly. I sat with him in art, and at lunch.'

'He's a pest,' I say. 'Seriously bugging. But then, I'm his sister – I would think that.'

Paul looks at me through long, sooty lashes, like he's seeing me for the first time. Lashes that long are wasted on a boy. You could practically sweep the floor with them.

'You look alike,' Paul considers. 'Same dark hair, same wide eyes.'

I get a fluttery feeling in my tummy, like the sort of lurching sensation you get when you drive over a humpback bridge and just about lose your breakfast.

'Hey, you two,' Joey calls back over her shoulder. 'We're thinking up names for the kittens. Any ideas?'

'Scrappy, Dusty and Scruff?' Paul offers. 'Because you found them in the dustbins, y'know?'

'Not bad,' Joey considers. 'I was thinking, something like Kit, Kat and Koko!'

'You want to name one of the kittens after my brother?' I wail. 'Joey, you can't. No way.'

'I was thinking more of the chocolate bar,' Joey admits. 'You love KitKats, Hannah. They're your favourite.'

'I know, but . . .'

'OK,' Joey shrugs. 'Not Kit, Kat and Koko.'

We turn off the coast road and into the lane that leads down to Beachcomber Cottage. The breeze blowing up from the sea is bitingly cold, and the hedgerows are still shimmery with frost. I crunch over frozen puddles, my feet like slabs of ice.

'Buffy, Willow and Spike?' I suggest. 'After the old TV reruns?'

'Is that from the show with the vampires?' Joey asks. 'Don't think I want vampire cats.'

'I like Paul's idea,' Kit says. 'I mean, they are dustbin kitties, aren't they? You need a name that suggests junk, rubbish, decay.'

'Yeuww.' I grimace. 'Why, exactly?'

'Well, just *because*,' Kit shrugs with perfect boy-logic.

'They are pretty yukky,' Joey admits. 'Full of fleas and scabs.'

We can see Beachcomber Cottage now, the slate roof dusted with icing-sugar frost, the windows bright, the chimney trailing plumes of wood smoke. We file in through the rickety gate, nailed together from driftwood branches, beneath the spindly driftwood garden arch where a climbing rose, blackened with cold, hangs on for dear life. The winding concrete path is embedded with shells and pebbles and edged with upturned wine bottles in blue and green.

Joey marches into the porch, jangling the wind chimes made from shells and seaglass and pieces of bleached-out driftwood twigs that look like the bones of small animals.

'I've got it,' Joey tells us, pushing open the door. 'The names, I mean. What's our favourite TV show?'

'*The Simpsons*?' I say.

'Exactly.'

We head into the kitchen, where Jed is sitting at the scrubbed pine table, helping Mikey with some maths homework. Eva is at the Aga, stirring a vast pan of hearty soup. The kitchen is bright and warm and chaotic, like a farmhouse kitchen in a kids' storybook.

'Hi, Paul, kids,' Jed says. 'How did it go?'

'OK,' Paul shrugs. 'No problems.'

'Great,' Eva grins. 'It's a friendly school – you'll soon settle in.'

Paul looks sceptical, but nobody seems to notice except me.

Joey slaps the cardboard box down in the middle of the table. Inside, the kittens begin to squawk.

'What's in the box?' asks Jed.

Joey unfolds the lid, and everyone peers in. The kittens blink fiercely in the bright light of the kitchen, looking lost and startled and hopelessly cute.

'Meet Itchy, Scratchy and Krusty,' Joey says.

CHAPTER 4

For years, we have been a gang of two, Joey and me. We hang out together at school, at each other's houses, in the village, at the beach. Now, overnight, we are a gang of four.

Kit and Paul are always around. Wherever we go, they go too.

It's good to walk into the lunch hall at school and see that they've saved us a space at their table. It's good to sit in the cafe in Kirklaggan, sipping milkshakes and pretending we're on some kind of double date when actually we're not. It makes me feel grown-up; it makes me feel cool.

Mostly, we mooch around at Beachcomber Cottage, feeding the kittens, teasing them with a catnip mouse on a piece of string or a plastic ball with a bell inside it that jingles when it moves.

We take them to the vet and watch them disappear in a fog of white flea powder. They emerge pale and grey and slightly shocked. We learn that the tortoiseshell cat is female, the two tabbies male. Krusty, the scabby tortoiseshell, has an allergy to fleas, but that will clear up if we keep her bug-free. The vet says they are remarkably well considering their shaky start in life.

'They'll be fine,' he says. 'Well done, kids.'

The kittens grow round and sleek with regular feeds, and their fur grows silky and soft. They lose their fear and learn to trust us, licking our hands with sandpaper tongues, purring like tiny engines as we stroke their bellies, tickle their ears. They sleep in a basket Jed found in a skip, on a blanket made from crochet squares that Eva rescued from a long-gone jumble sale. Krusty stops living up to her name.

I plan ahead for a day when she will sleep on the end of my duvet at home, waking me up with an alarm-clock purr, but so far Mum isn't keen on the idea. She is immune to kitten charm. She can only think of flea powder and worming tablets and cat-litter trays, and she is not impressed.

I'm working on it. Slowly.

At least I know Krusty's safe at Joey's – who wouldn't be? Beachcomber Cottage is pure magic.

It reminds me of the witch's house in the fairy story, where everything is made of gingerbread and sweeties, except that here everything is made of driftwood and junk, all transformed into a kind of crazy, weirdo beauty.

The worktops are made of vast slices of wood with the bark still showing along the edge, and the cupboards are cobbled together from what look like old fish boxes and seaworn planks with handles made from old brass spoons and forks, beaten and bent into shape. *Oban fresh fish*, one cupboard door reads. *Portpatrick*, says another.

We sit round the kitchen table, perched on weirdo chairs made from big, curving branches of weathered driftwood, eating warm scones with big curls of butter and jam made from brambles Joey and I picked last year, from the hedgerows along the lane.

Outside, Kit and Mikey are playing footy in the pool of light from the kitchen windows. Kit is always Celtic and Mikey is always Rangers. Somehow, Rangers always win.

'Rangers are the *champions*!' Mikey roars, coming in to grab a scone.

'Nah,' Kit tells him. 'You're just on a lucky streak. Celtic are the best: everyone knows that.'

'But we won!' Mikey insists.

'Yeah, you won.'

I have watched my brother stand in the makeshift goal between the plum trees and leap dramatically for every ball Mikey sends his way. I have watched him shake his head and slap his leg and roll his eyes as one shot after another flies past him. He's OK, Kit. Sometimes.

Other times, he's a pain.

'What d'you think, Paul?' Kit asks now. 'Are you Celtic or Rangers? Green or blue?'

Paul puts down his sketchbook. 'I've told you,' he says. 'I'm not into footy. Celtic, Rangers, it makes no difference.'

'You *must* like one or the other,' Kit insists.

'Why must I?' Paul asks evenly.

'Because everyone does,' Kit shrugs. 'You lived in Glasgow, you *have* to have an opinion. Football runs in the blood up there.'

'Not for me.'

'I get it. You're into Queen of the South.'

'No. I'm just not into football, Kit,' Paul says slowly, spelling it out.

'Sheesh kebab!' says Kit. 'Sorr-ee!' He doesn't sound sorry at all.

Paul Slater is an alien species as far as Kit is concerned, but he's struck a deal and he won't go back on it. He's helping Paul to settle in because Joey asked him to. And, with Joey at least, he is making progress.

He can make her laugh, he can make her blush and he can even make her stand around on the sidelines watching him play footy in sub-zero temperatures. Grim, especially when Paul and I end up huddled either side of her, wondering which will come first, death by frostbite or death by boredom.

'Don't encourage him,' I warn Joey. 'He'll think you mean it. We'll never get shot of him.'

'Aw, but it's funny,' Joey responds. '*He's* funny. And – well, it's kind of flattering to know that he likes me. It's cool.'

'He doesn't give up easily,' I tell her, and Joey just smiles.

One day, we go swimming after school at the pool in Kirklaggan, Joey and Paul and Kit and me. Paul surprises everyone by being a brilliant swimmer. He's not into splashing around in the shallows like Joey, who screams every time someone threatens to get her hair wet. He doesn't want to chuck a ball around or practise underwater handstands like me. He's not even into waiting for the lifeguard to turn his back so that he can do a running depth-charge jump like Kit.

Paul's long swim shorts have seen better days, and he doesn't bother to take off the sweatbands on his wrists, but he slips into the water like he belongs there. He swims length after length of smooth, fast crawl, with occasional lazy lengths of breaststroke or backstroke.

'That's some speed you've got there,' Kit says. 'You're good.'

'Think so?'

'Totally. You'll have to tell Mr Thomson, the sports coach. He'll put you in the team, no hassle.'

'Nah,' says Paul. 'I just swim because I like it. I don't want to be in a team. I don't want to compete.'

'But you should!' Kit exclaims. 'Seriously! Our swim team is rubbish – they need you. It's a waste to just do it for fun.'

'Nah.'

Later, the lifeguard asks him if he'd be interested in training with the local swimming club, but Paul just shrugs and smiles and shakes his head.

'Sheesh. Such a waste of talent,' says Kit as we sit in the cafe in Kirklaggan later, smelling faintly of chlorine. 'Crazy.'

Paul just smiles and sips his milkshake.

'Have you ever swum for your school?' Kit wants to know. 'Or been in a swimming club? I mean, how did you get to be so good?'

'I just like it,' Paul says. 'When I was little, we lived on an island. It made sense to know how to swim, so Mum taught me – in the sea.'

'Hey, we swim in the sea too!' I tell him. 'The beach behind your cottage is really safe and clean. There are some strong currents further out, but it's fine if you stay by the shore.'

'I don't swim in the sea any more,' Paul frowns.

'Not at this time of year,' Joey laughs. 'There are probably whole icebergs out there right now.'

'Not at any time of the year,' Paul says. 'The sea is dangerous. You can't trust it. It's way more powerful than any of us know.'

'Scaredy-cat,' Kit says, grinning. Paul just shrugs.

'Where was the island?' I ask, stirring my milkshake with a straw. 'You know, where you lived when you were little?'

Paul is silent for a while, like he doesn't want to answer. His eyes are kind of faraway.

'It was Mull,' he says softly, after a while. 'We lived in a cottage not far from the sea, just me and Mum and our cat. Splodge, she was called.'

'What happened?' Kit asks. 'How come you ended up in care?'

There's another silence, and Paul lets out a long, low sigh.

'Mum went away,' he tells us. 'She'd been depressed and she just went away one day, and never came back. I waited and waited, but she never came. Then a neighbour found me and called the social services and that was that. I've lived in three different foster homes and four different care homes since then.'

I'm biting my lip so hard I can taste blood.

'Oh, Paul,' Joey says. 'That's awful.'

'Sheesh,' says Kit. 'Sorry, mate.'

'It's OK,' says Paul. 'It's just the way it is. She was depressed, or she'd never have left me, I know that. She'll come back one day. Any time now, seriously. So you don't have to feel sorry for me, OK?'

Joey is looking down at the tabletop, tracing patterns in a patch of spilled sugar. Kit rakes a hand through his pool-damp hair, teasing it into spikes. Nobody can meet Paul's gaze.

'What happened to Splodge?' I make myself ask. 'What happened to the cat?'

'Dunno,' says Paul. 'I never saw her again.'

CHAPTER 5

My mum is not a cat person. Kittens are bad news, she says. They claw the furniture and climb up the curtains and do unspeakable things in the corner when you're not looking.

'You are not having a cat,' she says firmly. 'I'm sorry the poor thing was dumped, but you found it and rescued it and it has a good home now, with the Donovans. There's no way it's coming here.'

'Mu-um!' I appeal, but resistance is futile. Mum grabs a fluffy yellow duster and a can of furniture polish, and dusts her way around the living room, polishing away all traces of imaginary kitten.

'No, Hannah,' she says as she works. 'Really. No.'

Dad, hiding behind a newspaper, raises one eyebrow and shrugs, and I know I'm on my own here. I will not give up, though. I love Krusty and Krusty loves me, and one day we'll be together, I just know it.

Kit, of course, thinks differently.

He is out of bed at nine thirty on a Saturday morning, crunching along beside me through a light fall of snow towards Joey's house. Normally, earthquakes, volcanoes and full-on asteroid showers cannot part him from his quilt on a non-school day.

'You'll never get to keep that scabby cat,' he says sweetly. 'No chance.'

'Well, cheers, Kit.'

I used to think Kit was the coolest big brother in the world. He could do ollies and kick-flips on his skateboard, wheelies on his BMX, score shedloads of goals on the footy field. All that, and he was nice to me too. He'd ruffle my hair, share his bubblegum, help me with my maths homework, sneak into my bedroom at midnight to tell ghost stories, eat jam sandwiches and invent crazy games with my fluffy beanbag rabbit.

All that stopped when Kit turned twelve. Overnight, he decided that cool meant snotty. If I tried to say something funny, his smile was sneery and sarcastic. The last time he helped me with my homework, I got every single sum wrong and *see me* scrawled across the bottom of the page, and just last week I walked into my bedroom to find my ancient fluffy rabbit hanging from the window latch, its head in a noose.

Teenage brothers are no joke.

'You could stick up for me about Krusty,' I suggest.

'I *could*,' Kit agrees, in the same tone as if he were announcing that pigs might fly. 'What d'you make of this Paul kid, anyway?'

'He's cool.'

'Flaky, though,' Kit says. 'I can't work him out. The lads at school don't like him much.'

'Why?' I ask, anxious. 'What's he done?'

Kit drags his glove along the top of a wall, collecting a handful of snow. He cradles it in his palms, making a snowball.

'He hasn't done anything,' Kit says. 'That's the trouble. He won't play footy, he won't come to the skatepark with me and Murphy and Fergus and Tom . . .'

'He can draw, though,' I point out. 'He's brilliant at it. And he's the best swimmer I've ever seen!'

'That's another thing!' Kit huffs. 'Murphy's on the swim team – he tried to talk Paul into joining up, but he's just not bothered. That's pretty selfish, when you think about it. You'd think he'd try, y'know? You'd think he'd *want* to fit in.'

Kit hangs back, supposedly to tie a lace that's come undone. When I turn to see how he's doing, it's too late. The snowball hits me slap in the face, hard enough to make my eyes water.

Then I suss that there are more snowballs coming, and I turn and run all the way down the lane to Beachcomber Cottage. There's snow in my hair, making my scalp tingle, dripping icily down my neck.

As I skid in through the gate, I see that the entire Donovan family are outside. Jed is shovelling snow off the driveway while Joey, Paul, Mikey and Eva are building a snowman. Already it is a Donovan-type creation, with fir cones for buttons and twigs for arms.

I flounder over to them, calling for a united attack on Kit.

'Snow war!' yells Joey, letting the first missile fly. It catches Kit on the kneecap, and he laughs, ducking behind a bush. We pelt him until he's caked with snow, hair dripping, ears scarlet.

'Snow massacre, more like,' Eva says. 'I'll go and put the kettle on for hot chocolate.'

'D'you surrender?' I shout, and Kit calls back that he'll never give in, not while there's breath left in his body. He retreats to make more snowballs, and Mikey, the traitor, runs off to help. Paul and Joey and I swoop about, scraping up more snow, piling up missiles.

'Now!' Joey squeals. 'Go for the kill!'

Joey's first snowball hits Kit in the stomach, but

he runs forward and grabs her by the waist, whirling her round and round. Paul pelts Kit with a quick volley of snowballs, while I sneak up behind him and manage to shove a snowball right down the back of his hoodie. Kit roars, dropping Joey into the snow and shoving me down.

I fall hard, winded, and lie still for a moment, catching my breath. When I haul myself up, face stinging with the cold, Joey is getting to her feet too, brushing the snow from her clothes and hair, trying to hold Mikey at arm's length.

A few feet away, Paul lies pinned to the ground while Kit sits astride him, crumbling snow on to his face.

'C'mon, Slater, you muppet,' Kit pants. 'Fight back! You're meant to struggle!'

'It's OK. You win,' Paul says breathlessly. His hat has come off and his hair is matted with snow, but his cheeks are glowing. His long lashes are crusted with snow.

Kit lowers his last snowball and stands up, brushing down his jeans.

'Muppet,' he says, shaking his head. 'C'mon, let's go in.'

Eva's made hot chocolate for everyone. She and Jed go through to the workshop, and Mikey follows, leaving us alone in a steamy kitchen, our wet shoes and coats lined up by the Aga.

Joey's favourite Good Charlotte tracks roar out from a CD player perched on top of a huge, scarlet fridge. Jed says the fridge is fifty years old and he found it in a skip, and I believe him.

Once, Jed was driving Joey and me into town when we passed a skip by the side of the road, overflowing with cruddy bits of furniture. Jed stopped and made us get out to help drag big, ugly cupboards and bookcases into the back of the van. A month later, Jed had stripped the dark wood back to pale oak, made new handles from twisty driftwood sticks and stuck rows of larch cones along the edges of the bookcases. It all looked mysterious and elegant, like something a hobbit or an elf might own, and he sold the lot at a craft fair in Carlisle for hundreds of pounds. He's clever like that, Jed.

He and Eva make a living from the sea. They pick up driftwood, shells, seaglass, rope, and turn it into something new, something beautiful. Maybe a chair, a bench, a stool, or maybe a mirror, a treasure chest, a mobile. Weird, like Kit says, but wonderful too.

I feed the kittens. They can lap milk from a saucer now, and wolf down little servings of mashed-up tinned meat. Krusty climbs up my body like she's scaling Everest, then curls softly round my neck like half a fur collar. I can hear her low, rasping purr as she drifts into sleep, and feel her tummy stretched tight as a drum, soft as silk.

Joey and Kit are playing chess. She's winning, but sneakily, trying to look baffled when Kit makes a good move, pretending to think hard when really she has the whole game boxed off. When you first play Joey at chess, you think you're winning. Then you think it's an even match, and finally, as she mashes you to a pulp, you realize you never had a hope. Kit hasn't got to that stage yet. He's taking it seriously, showing off.

Paul is curled up in the window seat, sketching. Behind him, falling snow patterns the windowpane like lace. He keeps glancing over to the chess game, then back down to his sketchbook, totally absorbed.

'What you drawing, Muppet?' Kit asks.

'Miss Quinn reckons if I do lots of sketches of real people, my cartoon figures will get better, stronger,' Paul explains. 'So I am.'

'Aren't you a bit old for cartoons?' Kit asks, which is a bit rich coming from someone who still buys the *Beano* every week.

'Comic-book art is cool,' Paul argues. 'It's what I want to do, what I care about.'

'OK,' Kit shrugs. 'Just asking. I mean, you're not into the usual S2 stuff, are you? Footy, skateboarding, music, girls.'

'Leave him,' Joey says, sweeping Kit's queen off

the chessboard. 'We're all different, aren't we?'

'Some of us are more different than others,' Kit says darkly. 'So, Muppet, gonna show us your sketches?'

Paul throws the sketchbook down on the kitchen table. There's a sketch of Jed in his workshop, and Eva slumped in a driftwood chair. There's one of Mikey playing with his cars, me feeding Krusty with an ink-dropper, and Joey, hair sticking out at right angles, in her outsize blazer and frayed skirt.

'Not bad,' Kit admits. 'What about today's one, though? You were drawing us play chess, weren't you?'

'At the back,' Paul says quietly.

At the back of the sketchbook we find today's drawing of Kit looking down at the chessboard with big, dark eyes, his hair still mussed up from the snow war. It's better than the other drawings – softer, warmer, stronger. It makes Kit look almost beautiful.

'Wow,' I breathe.

'Don't like it,' Kit says. 'You've made me look *girly*.'

'I don't think so,' Paul says.

Over the page there's a quick sketch of Kit in footy boots and games kit. Another, of Kit looking dreamy, his hair gelled into perfect spikes. A fourth, of Kit smiling, his whole face lit up from inside.

'Whoa,' says Joey.

Kit slams the book shut and chucks it across the table. It bounces off the chessboard, dislodging some pieces, then falls to the floor.

'What are you, some kind of *stalker*?' Kit demands. His voice is cold and hard, but it's shaking a little, and I know he's really angry.

'They're just sketches,' Paul protests. 'I like drawing.'

'Yeah, sure. Sketches of *me*. Well you can stop it right now, Muppet-boy. I've had enough.'

'I didn't mean –'

'You didn't mean what?' Kit flashes. 'Stay away from me. I mean it. No more drawings. OK?'

'OK.'

Paul picks his sketchbook off the floor, yanks open the Aga's fuel door and chucks the book inside. It's gone almost instantly, in a quick burst of flames, before anyone can protest. He sits down at the kitchen table, looking shell-shocked.

'Good riddance,' Kit says harshly. 'I'm bored with this place – I'm going up to Kirklaggan. Might get the bus to Dumfries. Anyone coming?'

There's a silence. Joey picks up the fallen chess pieces, trying to rearrange the board.

'I'll come, if you like,' Paul says.

'I'm not asking you, *Muppet*,' Kit snaps. He drags on his boots, his coat and gloves.

'I will, then,' Joey says casually. She pulls on an

extra pair of stripy socks, slips on the biker boots, and grabs her hat and coat.

'Joey, you can't,' I tell her, although she can, of course. I am not her mother; I am not her sister. I can't tell her what to do. She wouldn't listen anyway.

'What about the snow?' I say. 'It's really heavy now. You can't just go off in a blizzard. What will I say to Jed and Eva?'

Joey laughs. 'Tell them I'm learning to live a bit,' she says, and then she's out of the door, Kit's arm round her as they trudge up the garden path.

CHAPTER 6

Jed and Eva are not happy.

'She *can't* have gone to Dumfries, not in this,' Eva says, frowning. She rubs her hand across the windowpane as though it might help her to see better through the swirl of snow. 'She *wouldn't*. She wouldn't just go, without saying something.'

I think of Joey's parting shot, about learning to live a little, and press my lips firmly shut.

'They might turn back,' Paul says hopefully.

'I don't understand why they've gone in the first place,' Jed says. 'Kit came over to see you, Paul. Why would he just take off with *Joey?*'

'We had a fight.'

'A fight?' Eva looks at me as though I am

45

somehow responsible for keeping Kit in line. As if that were ever an option.

'A disagreement,' Paul corrects himself. 'Nothing serious. Kit decided to leave, and Joey went too.'

'So – did you and Joey fall out too?' Jed asks me.

'No.'

'But she's gone off and left you, without explaining why?'

I glance at the abandoned chess game, a few pieces still scattered across the table.

'I think Joey likes Kit,' I say quietly. It's like the whole idea of it only just occurred to me, but the minute I say it out loud I know it's the truth. Kit likes Joey, that's old news. But Joey likes *Kit*?

Where does that leave me?

'Well, he's a nice enough kid . . .' Jed says.

'I mean, I think she *likes* him,' I explain. 'Y'know? And he likes her.'

There's a silence.

'She's too young,' Eva frowns.

'This is crazy,' Jed says. 'Dumfries is twenty-five miles away. On a day like this!'

'What if the buses stop running?' Eva panics.

'The snow's not that bad,' I whisper. 'Is it?'

'Would they go back to your place, Hannah?' Eva appeals. 'I could ring your mum.'

'Worth a try.'

But Joey and Kit are not at my place, and Eva's

phone call just gets Mum and Dad all worried. Dad says he'll take a walk around the village to see if he can find them, and Eva promises that I'll be dropped home safely as soon as Jed has the van on the road.

She drifts back to the window, pressing her face against the lace-patterned glass. She is not the kind of person who worries about school uniform or black lipstick, biker boots or stripy hair, but she is worried now. Her face is pale and her brow is crumpled.

'It'll be OK,' I say, but she doesn't seem to hear me.

'It's my fault,' Paul mumbles. 'My fault they've gone.'

I guess maybe it is Paul's fault – that thing with the sketchbook was pretty freaky. Why so many pictures of Kit? If they were of me, I'd be embarrassed, but happy too. Kit is embarrassed and seriously hacked off. I know he is finding Paul hard work, and I have a feeling this may just kill the friendship dead.

'I think you made Kit feel uncomfortable,' I say carefully. 'All those pictures of him.'

'It's just that he's in my class, y'know?' Paul shrugs. 'He's my friend. He's always around. It was just easy to draw him.'

Maybe, maybe not. I look at Paul's sad eyes and

I want to say something to make it better for him.

'Kit overreacted,' I tell him, pulling on my coat and boots. 'They were just pictures, weren't they? And Joey shouldn't have gone at all. Don't worry – they're probably in Dumfries, holed up somewhere warm and dry, eating pizza.'

'I've wrecked everything,' Paul says gloomily. 'Kit won't want to know me now.'

'He will,' I say, but I'm not so sure.

'No way. And now they're missing, and it's all my fault.'

'Don't worry,' I say, squeezing his arm with one mittened hand. 'They'll be fine. It'll all work out.'

Jed calls from the doorway that he's got the van running, so I grab my hat and scarf and head out into the storm.

Kit sneaks in the back door, some time after seven. He is halfway up the stairs when Dad collars him.

'Where have you been?' Dad wants to know. 'That poor girl's family are worried sick. What are you playing at?'

'I'm not playing,' Kit says.

'Where were you?'

'We went to Dumfries,' Kit snaps. 'I told Hannah. What's the big deal?'

'It was snowing,' Mum says. 'We were worried.'

'You don't usually worry,' Kit points out. 'Some

days, I'm out in Kirklaggan with Murphy, Fergus and Tom till past ten at night. You've never said anything before.'

'Joey's parents –'

'– act like she's still four years old,' Kit says. 'That's not my problem.'

'I think it might be,' Dad says. 'You're older than her. You should be more responsible. Let people know where you are, what you're doing.'

Kit shrugs. 'Right now, I'm going upstairs to my room,' he says. 'Is that OK with everyone?'

'Not really, no,' Dad huffs.

'Tough.' Kit turns his back and climbs the stairs, and we hear his door slam shut.

Dad goes kind of pink and his lips set into a hard, tight line. He stomps into the living room, resisting the temptation to slam the door himself. I watch him chewing his lip as he battles with his temper.

'At least he's found a nice girl,' Mum says brightly. 'A bit offbeat, Joey, but very polite. He's growing up, our Kit.'

'He'll never see fourteen the way he's going,' Dad mutters darkly. 'Cheeky little git.'

Kit is grounded for a month. He is not allowed to hang out with his mates, he is not allowed to see Joey and, most importantly of all, he is not to set foot in Beachcomber Cottage.

'This is *so* unfair,' Kit grumbles later, when I tell

him about the ban. I've smuggled him up cold pizza and chips left over from teatime, but there has to be a trade-off. I want information, hard facts.

'Shouldn't have cheeked Dad, should you?' I tell him. 'Boy, is he mad. You're lucky it's only a month.'

'They're making way too much of it,' Kit protests. 'I went into Dumfries with Joey. How come the world has such a problem with that?'

'Is she your girlfriend now?' I ask.

Kit shrugs. 'Maybe. You'd better ask her.'

'D'you want her to be?'

'You know I do, Hannah. That's not a crime, is it?' Kit says. 'I like Joey. A lot. It's Paul Slater I have a problem with.'

'He didn't mean any harm.'

'The kid's a nightmare, Hannah,' Kit huffs. 'I've tried to help him fit in, be his mate. What does he do? Gets all weird and creepy on me, like some kind of headcase stalker.'

'He was only drawing!'

'Yeah. Well, if he comes near me with a pencil again, I'll break his fingers. You can tell him that from me, OK? It's his fault, this whole mess.'

I flop down on the end of Kit's bed and watch him wolfing down dried-up old pizza. He doesn't tell me to get lost like he normally would. His open wardrobe reveals a rail of neatly ironed hoodies, black T-shirts and jeans shaped like potato sacks.

On his desk, next to the PlayStation 2, sit body spray, hair gel and a brand of shower gel that claims to make skinny, spotty boys irresistible to women.

'Paul is part of Joey's family right now,' I remind Kit. 'You can't just drop him.'

'Watch me.'

'Joey won't like that,' I warn, but Kit just shrugs. He is smiling slightly to himself, like he knows way better than I do what Joey will or will not like. He reaches over to his coat pocket, takes out a fat, white package and hands it to me.

'Got you this,' he says carelessly. 'In town.'

I unwrap a squashed, greasy doughnut with pink sugar sprinkles. When we go to Dumfries as a family, we always buy hot doughnuts from the bakery in the high street. This is my favourite kind.

'Not as good cold,' he says regretfully.

'Still yummy, though. Thanks, Kit.'

'No problem. Thanks for the pizza.'

I grin, biting into my doughnut. Maybe Joey will be a good influence on my brother. Maybe he will go back to being kind and thoughtful, the way he was before puberty got in the way.

'Do you think Joey will be in trouble for today?' he asks me. 'Were Jed and Eva mad?'

I pull a scary face. 'Kit,' I tell him, 'seriously. You don't want to know.'

*

Much later, when I'm almost asleep, my mobile goes off somewhere on the other side of the room. Joey downloaded an old Good Charlotte song 'Riot Girl' as the ringtone. It is not the kind of ringtone you really want to hear at eleven forty-five on a Saturday night when you are just a whisper away from sleeping, and it sends me scrambling across the room in a kind of panic.

Joey doesn't have a mobile because Jed and Eva think the radio waves scramble your brain or something. Possibly they would reconsider if they happened to find one in a skip. They could always decorate it with seashells and clumps of seaweed to neutralize the bad vibes.

I jump back into bed and press the call button.

'Hannah? It's me, Joey.'

'Hi! Are you OK? What happened?'

'Oh, Hannah, I had a fantastic time. We got the bus to Dumfries – it took forever, because of the snow. Kit knows all these really cool places. I bought a T-shirt down on the Whitesands and a pair of red fishnets for school –'

'Joey,' I interrupt her. 'What did Jed and Eva say? Aren't you in trouble?'

'Oh, well, sort of,' she admits. 'They're not happy, but what can they do?'

'Ground you for a month, like Dad did to Kit?' I suggest.

'No way!' Joey howls. 'Poor Kit! That's terrible. I thought Jed and Eva were bad. I had two solid hours of lectures and warnings, but I said sorry, and I promised I'd never go off again without telling them where I was going.'

'Jammy pig,' I say. 'How come you always get away with murder?'

'Must be my natural charm,' Joey says, giggling. 'How's Paul?'

'He's OK. Kit's pretty hacked off with him, though. Thinks he's some kind of stalker.'

'Kit overreacted,' I say firmly. 'Paul just likes to draw.'

'Whatever,' Joey says. 'Kit just got spooked out, that's all. It was a bit weird, you have to admit.'

I'm not about to admit anything, so I chew my lip and ask the question that's been bugging me all day. 'Are you going out with my brother?'

There's a long pause, and I hear Joey sigh. 'Will you be mad if I say yes?' she says.

'Will it make any difference?' I counter.

'Not really. I like him, Hannah. He's really cute and funny and cool.'

'Yeuww. I don't want to hear this.'

'OK. No problem.'

There's another long pause, and then Joey breaks the silence. 'Thing is, Hannah, could you let me speak to him?' she asks. 'I just wanted to thank him for today, let him know I'm OK. I had to wait till it was late – I didn't want Jed and Eva listening in. I thought your mobile would be more private and stuff. So if it's OK . . .'

I tiptoe across the landing and sneak into Kit's room. He jolts awake when I switch the light on, looking like a startled rabbit.

'It's for you,' I whisper, holding out the mobile, and his face lights up like a kid on Christmas morning.

I close the door behind me, creep back across the landing and into bed. I am pleased, really, for Kit and Joey, but it's been a long day, a weird day, an exhausting, confusing, crazy day.

I pull the covers up over my head and press my face into the pillow, and I wonder why my throat is aching with tears I'm too proud to cry.

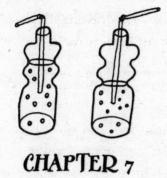

CHAPTER 7

I guess I'm just not ready to lose Joey to some spotty, skinny boy. It doesn't help that it's my own brother – it's not like Joey and I can talk into the small hours about how cute he is. Please.

'It's amazing,' she says for the forty-second time this week, as we lean up against the cast-iron radiators waiting for Kit's class to come out from French. 'I mean, all those years and I just never really *saw* him before, you know?'

'Whatever,' I shrug.

'He's a great kisser. Really strong lips.'

'Joey! Too much information, seriously.'

At this moment, Mr McKenzie stalks past and casts an outraged glance at Joey's Royal Stewart tartan minikilt, draped with chains. It is barely visible beneath the hem of her ratbag blazer, which may account for Mr McKenzie's purple scrunched-up face. Any minute now, there will be steam coming out of his ears.

'Miss Donovan,' he chokes out. 'What . . . is . . . *this*?'

He flicks a gnarled and quivering hand towards the tartan skirt, and Joey springs to life and does a little twirl for him.

'Sir, I know it's not uniform,' she says sweetly. 'I know that, and I'm sorry. But we are a Scottish school, and I'm a Scottish girl. We're studying Scottish history and learning Robert Burns's poems in English, and you're always telling us to be proud of our heritage, aren't you? So I thought that, under the circumstances –'

'You thought *wrong*,' Mr McKenzie roars. 'That skirt must go!'

'What, now, sir?' Joey blinks.

Mr McKenzie backs away, suddenly pale. 'Not *now*, you insolent girl,' he says shakily. 'You know fine well what I mean. No more kilts, Miss Donovan. And you're in detention – for a week!'

As Mr McKenzie disappears round the corner, a small roar of applause breaks out behind us. Kit and his mates have been watching from the classroom doorway. Murphy, Tom and Fergus melt away, leaving Kit to wander up to Joey. He brings a packet of sweets out of his blazer pocket and hands them to her. Love Hearts.

I turn away, suddenly in need of fresh air.

Outside, the playground is a muddle of football games. Small knots of girls huddle on the edges, gossiping, catching up on homework or reading magazines. Beyond them I spot Paul Slater, sitting alone on a low piece of wall beside the music block. Paul has been alone all week – in class, in the lunch hall, in the playground. He's probably feeling worse than I do.

I walk over to him, watch him close a small black sketchbook and slide it into his pocket as he sees me approach. He slips a pencil behind his ear and grins at me from behind the toffee-coloured hair.

'OK, Hannah. No Joey today?'

'She's with Kit,' I tell him. 'Surprise, surprise. I kind of got the feeling that three was a crowd.'

'Ouch,' Paul says. 'That's two of us out in the cold, then.'

'Kit still hacked off about the drawings?' I ask.

'Ever so slightly. I just thought – at the start – I thought it might work out OK. Should have known.'

'Kit's a pain,' I tell him. 'Don't stress, you'll make other mates.'

'I'm not so good at all that stuff,' Paul admits. 'I've always been more of a loner.'

'You don't have to be,' I say.

'Don't *worry*. I'm fine.'

'OK. See you in Miss Quinn's room at lunchtime?' I ask, throwing him a quick lifeline.

'Yeah, maybe.'

As I walk away, a football crashes up against the wall where Paul is sitting. Tom, Murphy and Fergus shout over. 'Kick us the ball back, Muppet!'

I watch over my shoulder as Paul walks over, scoops up the ball and throws it back into the playground. In seconds, it bounces back again.

'Oi, Muppet!'

Paul picks up the ball and throws it back a second time, but Murphy slams it straight back over. This time it hits Paul on the leg, hard. He looks faintly hacked off, but chucks the football back again.

Instantly, Murphy slams it back. I stop walking and turn to watch.

'*Kick* it back, Muppet,' Murphy shouts. 'Only girls throw. Can't you kick?'

Paul looks at Murphy for a long moment, his gaze clear and steady. Then he turns to get the ball, hooking it with the toe of his boot. He glances briefly at Murphy, Tom and Fergus, then kicks the ball hard in the opposite direction. It ricochets off the music room, scuffs across the grass and bounces through a knot of S2 girls before disappearing behind the science block.

Paul Slater walks away, not looking back. He

doesn't see the look of fury on Murphy's face. He doesn't know he's made an enemy.

I cannot stand another five minutes of watching Kit and Joey feed each other bits of sandwich and sips of orange juice across the lunch table.

'Fancy going up to the art room?' I ask Joey, but she just mouths 'later' and turns her back so she can listen to Kit describe the plot of last night's *Simpsons'* episode, practically word for word.

Nightmare. My smart, sassy and sometimes scary best mate is turning into a fluff-brained, lovesick gimp. When Kit is around, nobody else exists for her. It's possible I am becoming invisible.

'I'm gonna go on up,' I tell her.

'Mmm.'

'There's a rumour going around that Benji from Good Charlotte will be there,' I say, testing to see if she's even listening. 'Miss Quinn invited him in to give a one-off workshop on non-permanent tattoos.'

'Right,' says Joey vaguely.

This proves it. I am officially invisible.

Room 15 is packed with the usual ragbag of kids. The ones who are into their art sit painting or doing strange, experimental stuff with wire and pliers and papier mâché. The ones who are avoiding the windswept playground lounge on desktops, chatting and adding the occasional scribble to a piece of classwork. The ones who are here because they have nowhere else to go, nobody else to be with, try the hardest to look busy.

Normally, I'm in the second category, looking for a warm place to hang out when the weather gets arctic. Today, though, I know I'm in with the losers, the loners. I fish my art folder out from the drawers and take out an unfinished still-life painting.

'Hi, Hannah.'

Paul Slater waves from the sink area, then wanders over to where I'm sitting. His sleeve-ends are damp from the sink, because he never bothers to push them up, but he doesn't seem to care. He sets a paint palette and water jar down on the table, and takes a huge comic-style happy families picture from his folder. Two smiling faces, a young woman and a little boy, arranged like a holiday snapshot.

'It's good,' I tell him. 'Is that your mum?'

'It's how I remember her, anyway,' Paul says with a shrug. 'I don't have any photos. Sometimes it's hard to remember, exactly.'

'Tough one.'

Paul fishes a glass bottle of something red and fizzy from his rucksack, pushing it across the table at me. It's one of those old-fashioned kinds of pop you can buy at the corner sweet shop opposite the school. Cherryade. It's sweet and cool and fizzy, with a flavour of long-ago summers.

'You OK?' Paul presses. 'You look sort of hacked off.'

'I'm invisible,' I tell him, holding up a hand to check whether it's transparent or not. 'It's happening slowly, but it's happening. Pretty soon, you won't see me at all.'

'What are you talking about?'

'Seriously,' I tell him. 'People can't see me. People can't hear me. I could disappear any minute.'

Paul Slater laughs. 'Have you been hanging around with Romeo and Juliet again?' he asks me. 'Don't take it personally. They wouldn't notice if there was an earthquake right next to them.'

'It feels like I'm losing my best mate,' I tell him. 'It hurts.'

'Yeah, I know,' he says sadly, and I remember that he does.

'Hey, we'll survive,' I grin. 'Won't we?'

'Definitely,' Paul says.

'Are you sure I'm not looking hazy to you?' I check. 'Kind of wishy-washy?'

'Not even slightly.'

We paint in silence for a while, and then Miss Quinn glides up beside us. 'No Joey today?' she asks.

'Joey's got a boyfriend,' I explain, trying the words out for size.

'Sweet!' Miss Quinn smiles.

'Er, no, not exactly!'

'Oh, well. I don't suppose it'll last forever.' She shrugs. 'How are those kittens getting along?'

'They're fine. They're eating solid food now, and they're huge – compared to when we found them, anyway. They're really clever too.'

'Almost house-trained,' Paul chips in. 'Except for when Itchy mistook Eva's handbag for the litter tray.'

'Scary,' says Miss Quinn.

'Very.'

Later on, in maths, I'm ploughing through a shedload of fractions. Joey, who loves maths (I told you she was weird), has finished and sits doodling hearts and skulls all over the back of her jotter in silver pen.

'Hey,' she whispers when Mr Ballantine turns his back to scrawl a few more sums on the blackboard. 'Was it just a rumour, then, about Benji from Good Charlotte?'

I blink at her. 'He was there, all right,' I say. 'He's much better looking in real life. You missed out.'

'Show me your tattoo, then!'

'I can't,' I say, my mouth twitching into a smile. 'It's in a very private place.'

'You wouldn't just be saying that?' Joey asks, her eyes laughing. 'To get your own back?'

'Would I lie about something that important?'

'Possibly, Hannah. Possibly. But if he were to turn up . . .'

'Mmm?'

'Would you get his autograph for me?'

I raise an eyebrow. 'Whatever would Kit say?' I tease her.

Joey rolls her eyes. 'Kit?' She laughs. 'Kit who?'

CHAPTER 8

On Valentine's Day, a lumpy black envelope arrives, delivered by hand, decorated with stars and spirals and little pawprints done in silver pen. There's no name on it, just a cute little cartoon of a face that's half cat, half human. It's pretty much a Joey-type stunt, right down to her cool silver pen.

Kit swoops on the envelope and rips it open, grinning from ear to ear like a chimpanzee. He takes out a four-finger KitKat and looks at it, frowning a bit.

'*Kit*Kat,' I point out. 'Geddit?'

'Oh. Oh, yeah. Cool.'

He unfolds a torn scrap of tracing paper with a pencil drawing of a heart on it, a cartoon cat face sketched on top. It has wide eyes and a cute, kittenish look. 'OK,' he says, still puzzled. 'Is it for me? Kit*Cat*?'

I peer over his shoulder. 'Looks like it,' I tell him. 'It's a home-made tattoo. You soak the tracing paper in water, then rub it on to your arm or whatever. Shall I show you?'

'Suppose so. I'd better put it on, hadn't I?'

'Think so.'

Kit rolls up his sleeve and I transfer the tattoo to his forearm. It looks good – I'm impressed. I wonder if Joey got Paul to help her with it? There's a little needle of jealousy that she didn't ask me, or even tell me about it.

On the bus, Kit captures Joey the moment she gets on. 'Sit with me,' he appeals. 'Just for today. Please?'

Joey shrugs at me and sits. I knew she would. I just thought it might take a little more persuasion. Well, *some* persuasion, anyway. But, no, Kit asks and Joey sits, it's that simple. Paul, coming up the aisle behind her, catches my eye.

'Seat taken?' he asks.

'Nah, go ahead,' I sigh. 'It's Valentine's Day, isn't it? Joey's busy getting slushy with KitKat over there.'

'KitKat?' Paul questions, flopping down beside me.

'Some people get valentine cards,' I explain. 'My

brother gets chocolate and a home-made tattoo –
Joey likes to be different.'

'Yeah? She sent him a tattoo and a KitKat?'

'Well, it wasn't addressed to him,' I admit, 'but
it's pretty obvious. *KitKat*, y'know? And the envelope
was all hearts and swirls, done in Joey's silver pen.'

'She's just given him a big card with a fluffy
heart on it too.'

'Yeuww.' I grimace. 'Kit's giving Joey this skull-
and-crossbones silver ring he got Tom to buy for
him in Dumfries. It's one she admired that day they
went off in the snowstorm, apparently. And he's
burned her a CD of all this punky stuff he
downloaded from the Net. It's taken him days.'

'He's thoughtful, your brother,' says Paul.

'Yeah, he's a regular dream boy,' I agree. 'So
kind, so helpful, so *friendly*.'

'He tried,' Paul shrugs. 'Don't blame him. It was
me that messed things up.'

I watch Kit scoffing the KitKat in big, greedy
bites and decide to blame him anyway.

Kit and Joey stay glued together all day, outside
of lesson times. They snuggle up so close in the
lunch hall, you'd just about need a chisel to prise
them apart. I give up on Joey and hide out in the
art room, washing palettes for Miss Quinn until
Paul appears with a bag of chips and a bottle of
Cherryade.

'You've been out to the chippy!' I cry, outraged. 'Not fair!'

'Better than that mush you get down in the lunchroom,' he says. 'I'll get you some tomorrow, if you like.'

'Please!'

'Hot food's not allowed in the classrooms,' Miss Quinn says, gliding up behind us. 'Give us a chip and I won't tell.'

'Go ahead,' Paul grins. We sit down and demolish the chips, then glug Cherryade straight from the bottle. Paul produces a KitKat from his pocket and offers me half.

'Why should Kit be the only one who gets to eat KitKats?' He grins. 'C'mon, Joey says they're your favourite.'

So we munch chocolate and talk and paint, and lunchtime slips by.

After school, I get off at Joey's stop and watch her waving as the bus – and Kit – disappear from view.

'It's so unfair that he's grounded,' Joey says, sulking.

'My heart bleeds for you,' I tell her, and she pinches me, hard, on the arm.

I have bought a tin of sardines for the kittens as a special Valentine's Day treat. I get to cuddle up with Krusty and eat a piece of Eva's treacle tart while Joey shows everyone her silver ring.

Mikey and Paul are helping Jed put the finishing touches to a cat flap in the kitchen door. It's not just any old cat flap. Jed has sliced a square out of the door and hinged on a little swing door made from an old fish-box he found on the beach. Now Mikey and Paul are edging it round with little twigs of driftwood bleached white from the ocean.

'There's a whole wide world out there,' Paul tells the kittens, 'full of adventure and fun. It's awesome, but you have to take care.'

'Don't get run over by a tractor,' Mikey warns.

Joey slips her new CD into the player on top of the fridge. Kit's first track is a Good Charlotte song.

'Oh, he's so cool,' she sighs. 'How did he know?'

'Joey, everyone in the school knows you're obsessed with Good Charlotte. It isn't exactly a secret!'

'Well, but he's just so thoughtful.'

'You are too,' I say, just so Kit doesn't sprout a halo and wings. 'You put a lot of effort into his valentine.'

'It took me ages to choose it,' Joey says. 'I went to three different shops.'

'No, I meant the tattoo. Remember when we first learnt to make tracing-paper tattoos from that face-painting book in primary school?'

'Hannah, what're you talking about?'

'You know, the cat tattoo you sent to Kit,' I say. 'Dur! And the KitKat too.'

Joey sits down at the table. 'I didn't send him that tattoo,' she says slowly. 'I thought he just did it himself. And I don't know anything about a KitKat.'

I blink. 'It had to be you,' I protest. 'It was in a black envelope, all decorated with stars and spirals in silver.'

'No, not me,' Joey says. 'I just gave him the card. I was playing it cool – I didn't know if he'd make a fuss of Valentine's Day or not. Kit must have another admirer.' Her eyes darken, and she looks a little lost.

'He thinks it was you,' I point out. 'We don't have to tell him any different.'

'No,' says Joey. 'No, we don't.'

But who else would send Kit a cat tattoo and a KitKat bar? I haven't a clue, and for once Joey hasn't either.

CHAPTER 9

'Dad is just so out of order,' Kit sulks. 'I have been grounded for two weeks and five days. Over what? Going out for a couple of hours with a girl I happen to like.'

'In a snowstorm, without letting anyone know where you were,' I add helpfully. 'Dad *might* have understood if you'd said sorry afterwards.'

'Yeah, well, I wasn't sorry,' Kit scowls. 'And it wasn't a snowstorm, just a few flakes of snow. I'm sick of being grounded. I'm sick of history homework and *EastEnders* and early nights. Watch and learn, Hannah. I won't be grounded much longer – wait and see.'

I watch, and I learn. Overnight, Kit turns into the perfect teenager. He tidies his room, carrying armfuls of festering T-shirts and socks to the washing machine and removing mouldering coffee cups that were last seen when I was about seven years old. He makes cups of tea for Mum and Dad and washes the dishes without being asked. He even hoovers the living-room carpet before school.

'It won't work,' Dad tells him sternly. 'You're still grounded.'

'I know,' Kit shrugs. 'I deserve it. But I just want you to know I've learned my lesson.'

'Hmphh,' says Dad. Kit picks wilted snowdrops from the garden and gives them to Mum, then washes the car and polishes it till it gleams.

'Don't you think we've been a bit hard on him?' Mum asks, arranging the snowdrops in a tiny vase.

'No, I don't,' Dad retorts. 'He stays grounded. He'll thank me for it in the end.'

Kit waves cheerily from a stepladder in the hallway, where he is dusting the light fittings. I haven't seen him this helpful since his bob-a-job days with the Cub Scouts, when he cleaned the kitchen floor so well he broke the mophead.

'He's growing up, Jim,' Mum says thoughtfully. 'He didn't mean to cause all that fuss and trouble. He's fallen for Joey and he wanted to spend some time with her. It was a misunderstanding, really.'

'He's too young to get mixed up with girls,' Dad growls.

'Oh, Jim, it's not girls, it's *Joey*,' Mum says.

'Exactly. Next thing we know, he'll have his tongue pierced and his hair dyed purple. She's odd, that girl.'

'What rubbish! She's been Hannah's best friend for years, and there haven't been any problems,' Mum says fairly. 'Joey is very well-mannered.'

'Odd,' says Dad.

Kit, listening from the stepladder in the hallway, grins with delight, and shakes his duster out all over my head.

Cups of coffee and shiny-clean cars don't soften Dad, but Kit sticks at it. He cleans the windows, making them so smeary Mum has to do them again, rearranges the CDs so Dad can't find anything and cooks a totally inedible supper, involving raw chips, lukewarm baked beans and charred steaks. He does it all with a cheerful, smiling face with just the right amount of penitence mixed in.

On Saturday morning, Dad pulls the curtains wide to find Kit has emptied out the potting shed right across the lawn and is sorting it into boxes and bin bags. He begins to weaken.

'Kit!' he roars through the window. 'What are you doing? That's *my* stuff you're messing with.'

'I know, Dad,' Kit says brightly. 'I'm doing it for you. Imagine how good it'll be to have everything tidy, know where everything is!'

'I *do* know where everything is,' Dad grumbles. 'At least, I did. It'll take me ages to get everything straight now. Put it back – and stop this helping-out business. I'm sick of it.'

'But, Dad, I'm trying to show you how sorry I am!'

'I believe you,' Dad huffs. 'But I want you to stop now.'

'Dad, I'm just being helpful. It's not a problem. And, after all, there's nothing else for me to do now that I'm grounded!'

Dad slams the window shut and Kit hauls the boxes and bin bags of junk back into the potting shed for Dad to sort out. He wanders into the house, whistling.

'How about a big fry-up?' he asks, pulling a tin of pineapple chunks and a punnet of tomatoes out of the cupboard. 'Do we have any sausages?'

'Kit, love, you don't need to bother. I was going to make scrambled eggs,' Mum says with an anxious expression on her face.

'No bother, Mum,' Kit says brightly. 'I can do eggs. No hassles.'

Dad groans and goes outside to inspect the potting-shed disaster, and Kit winks at me. 'Trust me,' he whispers, 'it'll all be over by lunchtime. Teatime at the latest.'

'Hope so,' I tell him, eyeing the egg-and-pineapple

mixture Kit is whisking up, and helping myself to cereal.

Over at Beachcomber Cottage, Joey is wallpapering her room with black plastic bin bags. The wallpaper paste doesn't work so well – the rectangles of black stick for a while, then slither down the wall leaving trails of slime. We have to wipe the walls with a duck-shaped sponge from the bathroom, throw the soggy black stuff out and start again using Eva's staple gun.

'They do know you're doing this,' Paul asks, 'don't they? Jed and Eva?'

'Of course they do,' Joey scoffs. 'It's freedom of expression, isn't it?'

'Right.'

We get one wall covered, but there are only a few bin bags left and we're running out of staples.

'Think I'll leave it there,' Joey decides. 'I might get black fur-fabric for this wall, and tinfoil for that one, and the last wall can just be a great big poster collage. What d'you think?'

'Sounds good,' Paul shrugs, pouring out mugs of Cherryade. He is getting addicted to the stuff. 'Sure you don't want any driftwood sculptures or seashell mobiles? A lampshade made of seaweed and starfish, perhaps?'

'No, thank you. I had an idea for the lampshade,

though.' Joey cuts the last few bin bags into fringes and staples them on round her existing lampshade. The room is instantly dimmer, throwing spiky, flickering shadows across the walls. 'D'you think I should tie-dye my sheets and pillowcase black?' she ponders, but Eva shouts us to come downstairs and the room makeover comes to an abrupt end.

Standing in the kitchen, half hidden behind a vast bunch of yellow daffodils, is Kit. Mikey is clinging on to him like a limpet, grinning madly.

'Hi, Joey,' Kit says shyly. 'Thought I'd call over.'

'Kit! You're not grounded any more!'

Kit looks at his watch. 'As of twenty-five minutes ago,' he tells us. 'I was giving the fence a coat of creosote, and it dripped all over those nice beige chinos Mum got me last year . . .'

'Shame,' Eva says innocently.

'Yes, wasn't it?' Kit beams. 'Anyway, Dad said I'd been so helpful, and he knew how sorry I was and all, so he lifted the ban and here I am! I brought these for you, Eva, to say sorry for all the trouble and worry I caused.' He offers her the daffodils. I wonder how Mum will feel when she realizes her flower beds have been vandalized.

'Kit, you shouldn't have,' Eva says, but you can tell she's pleased. 'There's no hard feelings, really. We've all missed you being around, haven't we? Mikey has, and Paul.'

Kit nods and looks over at Paul, but can't quite meet his eye.

'Joey especially,' Eva grins.

'Mum!' Joey huffs. 'I haven't! I see him all the time, on the bus, at school, everywhere! There's no getting away from him!'

'No,' Kit grins. 'There isn't . . .'

He untangles himself from Mikey and flings an arm round Joey's shoulder, and I realize now that there's nowhere left at all where I can escape from the slushy waking nightmare that is Kit and Joey. I wish I could be happy for them, but I'm not. I'm really, really not.

I fish Krusty out of the cat basket and bury my face in her fur. I know that if I don't get out of this kitchen fast I will be crying like a little kid. I sniff hard, inhaling a kitteny, warm-milk and fur smell, and put Krusty down, wiping my eyes with the back of my hand.

'Anyone want ginger cookies?' Eva is calling, although Mikey has wandered off to find a football and Paul is curled up in the window seat, reading, and Joey and Kit are on the Planet Slush and therefore oblivious to everything.

I grab my coat from the hallway and slip out of the kitchen door. The driftwood cat flap makes a swish-swish noise as I click the door closed, but nobody notices I've gone, not even Krusty.

CHAPTER 10

Beachcomber Cottage sits right on the edge of the Solway coast, as though it just washed up on the shore like an especially gorgeous piece of driftwood. To the right a rocky headland juts out into the sea, while to the left the beach snakes away behind me, stretching back towards the distant harbour in Kirklaggan.

Out in the bay sits Seal Island, a tiny chunk of rock, grass and sand, glistening in the water. We used to call it Treasure Island and pretend a gang of cut-throat pirates lived there instead of just seals and gulls and long-necked cormorants.

I head out across the scrubby old strip of field at the back of Beachcomber Cottage, down to the beach. There's a rowing boat upside down next to the field wall, an ancient, weathered, grey thing that Jed used to take us out in. We'd go for picnics to Seal Island, and fishing expeditions where we used to try to catch mackerel with cotton line and silver chocolate wrappers as bait. We never caught a thing. The oars lie askew on the grass, abandoned.

We've played on this beach every summer since I can remember, Joey and me, being sailors and smugglers and castaways. We've had beach barbecues with Jed and Eva and Mikey, made bonfires from driftwood and toasted marshmallows in the flames. We've spent hours swimming here, building sandcastles that get washed away with the tide.

I've been out here hunting for driftwood too – hauling branches up to the cottage, searching through the tideline for anything weird or wonderful. I've gathered gulls' feathers, pebbles, hunks of seaweed and broken glass polished by the waves into smooth, frost-bright jewels. I've seen dead jellyfish like fallen stars, razor shells, mussels and shells like tiny pink fingernails. I have found old shoes, plastic bottles, broken toys and once an old wooden-framed sofa that Joey and I dragged up beyond the tideline and used for sunbathing all summer long.

The beach has a way of shrinking your problems down to size. As I walk out to the sea, the rain begins, a soft drizzle that pelts my cheeks and turns my hair to rat's tails. I let the churning waves crash over my shoes in a froth of white, while the wind lifts my hair and whips it around my face.

I am not proud of how I feel. My best friend is in love with my brother and it makes me feel left out, unwanted. Self-pity seeps through my body. It's an ugly feeling, like barbed wire inside you.

I lift my head and wipe my eyes, then turn and walk along the edge of the water, as far as the headland. By the time I reach the sliver of land that juts out into the bay, I am shivering with cold. I stand looking out to Seal Island for a while, watching the surf break above the dark, rolling waves. White horses, Eva said once, pointing at the surf, and I'd watched the sea for hours on end hoping to see magical horses rise out of the water.

I still hope, sometimes, with that little part of me that wants to believe in magic.

'Hey!'

There's a shout behind me, and I turn to see Paul picking his way along the tideline, stopping to pick up the occasional shell. I wave, pulling the hood of my coat a little tighter against the rain, tucking the rat's tails back out of sight. My face is wet, but with rain, not tears, and if my eyes are red it could easily be the salt spray that's made them that way. I walk along the tideline towards him.

'Hey,' I greet him. He's grinning, the toffee curls

plastered flat against his head, green eyes wide.

'When did you sneak off?' he asks me. 'I didn't notice.'

'No,' I agree. 'Nobody did.'

'You're wrong – someone noticed. Someone followed.'

I look around, but we're alone on the beach. Paul sticks a hand inside his coat and pulls out a damp scrap of tortoiseshell fur.

'Krusty!' I squeal. 'Paul, she shouldn't be this far from the cottage! It's too wet, too cold. She's too young!'

'Don't blame me,' Paul shrugs. 'She didn't ask permission, just dragged herself out of Jed's new cat flap. I heard the door swing shut, and I couldn't see her, so I grabbed my coat and went outside. I looked everywhere – found her right down by the edge of the sand. She'd tracked you all the way.'

'She . . . what?'

'She followed you, Hannah,' Paul repeats. 'Some kitten, yeah?'

'Oh!' I reach out for Krusty and she clambers into my arms and up on to my shoulders. My hood falls back, and she settles herself round my neck, her favourite position. I can feel her purring like a small lawnmower, burrowing under my hair, her fur like silk.

There's a warm feeling inside me, and the

barbed-wire jags don't hurt as much any more. We trail back up across the sand, stopping beside a tumbledown stretch of old sea wall. The sand forms a little hollow there, protected on both sides by scrawny tufts of marram grass and gorse.

'Why did you take off?' Paul asks.

I shrug, looking back at the water, my eyes fixed on the horizon. 'Kind of felt out of place,' I tell him. 'My brother, my best mate – it feels a bit awkward, somehow. I don't like it.'

'Yeah, tough one.'

Paul sits down in the sandy hollow, and I huddle down to join him. It's sheltered there, out of the wind and the rain. We lean our backs against the old sea wall and watch Krusty leaping about in the sand, stalking an old crisp packet that's fluttering through the marram grass.

'They don't mean to hurt you,' Paul says. 'They're just so wrapped up in each other.'

'I know,' I say helplessly. 'It's stupid to feel this way. I just keep thinking – well, why them? Of all the girls in the world, Kit has to pick my best friend. I just wish . . .'

'What?'

'Well, that things could go back to the way they were before, when all four of us were friends. It's like, since they've got together, everything is messed up.'

'Tell me about it,' Paul sighs.

'You never get upset,' I say. 'It must be hard for you – I mean, I've seen how Kit treats you now. I know they've all dropped you, Fergus and Murphy and Tom, but you don't let it get to you. I wish I could be like that.'

Paul stares into the distance, silent. He wipes his eyes a couple of times with his coat sleeve, but his lips are set hard.

'Even when you feel like dirt,' he says at last, 'you can't let them see it. You have to put on a brave face. You can't let them win.'

I stare at Paul. 'He *did* hurt you, didn't he?' I exclaim. 'Kit. The loser.'

'No,' Paul argues. 'He didn't mean anything. He's cool, your brother.'

'I used to think that. Not any more.' I look out at Seal Island and the ocean beyond, and the wind whips my hair across my face and hides the tears that threaten to mess up my don't-care expression.

'Hey, you've got to get over this,' Paul tells me. 'Life's too short to be gloomy and sad. You've got to dump the bad feelings, lose them.'

'Yeah, but how?' I ask, watching Krusty tearing chunks out of a strip of seaweed.

'When I feel bad, I come down here and think,' Paul says. 'There's a kind of power about the sea, a sort of magic.'

'Yeah, yeah,' I say scornfully, but I'm listening. Paul gets up, picking up a couple of small rocks.

'You could bury your problems under the sand,' he suggests, 'or write a wish at the water's edge and let the tide take it away. You could write a message in a bottle . . .'

'Have you ever done that?' I ask.

'Maybe,' he says. 'When Mum left, I used to think that if I could just get a message to her, she'd come back, sort everything out.'

'D'you still think that?'

'Don't know,' Paul considers. 'It was a few years back, and I didn't have a beach to work with – I threw the bottle into the River Clyde. It has to be worth a try, though.'

'I guess.'

'Anyway,' he says, brightening up, '*this* kind of beach magic definitely works. You think about your problems, then find a rock or a stone to stand for each one. Choose it carefully – picking the right one is important. As you pick it up, your problem passes over into the stone, and then . . . well, you just chuck that stone as far out to sea as you possibly can. The sea will take your problems far, far away.'

'You reckon?' I laugh.

'Yeah, I reckon!' Paul says, and he hurls his stones out across the rolling sea. 'Sorted!'

I stand up and look around, then pick up two

smooth, flat stones that fit in the palm of my hand. I shut my eyes tight and try to visualize all my Kit-problems seeping into one, all my Joey-problems flowing into the other. Then I walk down to the water's edge, Krusty leaping at my heels, and skim the stones out over the water. Joey's stone skips twice before it falls under the waves, Kit's three times, which isn't bad on the open sea on a blustery day like this. I feel lighter, better. Perhaps I just have a strong imagination.

'Good skimming,' Paul says. 'I'm rubbish at that.'

'It's all in the arm movement,' I tell him, and we skim stones for twenty minutes or so, until Paul has got the technique sorted. I scoop up Krusty, the fearless, salty sea cat, and put her in the hood of my jacket, and we walk back up to Beachcomber Cottage, laughing.

CHAPTER 11

First thing on Monday morning, I am lounging aimlessly against the wall near the school kitchens, while Joey and Kit loiter nearby, giggling and whispering and holding hands. I am trying to develop a strong stomach, so I blank them out. It's too early in the morning for this amount of mushy stuff.

I am adding a few finishing touches to my map of Roman Britain when I see Miss Quinn coming up from the car park with armfuls of African fabric, a Swiss cheese plant and a bundle of hazel twigs complete with catkins. The hazel twigs are trailing behind as she wrestles the load into submission.

'Need a hand, Miss?' I ask.

'Oh, Hannah, that would be wonderful,' she

beams. 'I think maybe I needed to make two journeys.'

I rescue the hazel twigs and the Swiss cheese plant, following her across the courtyard and up the stairs to the art room.

'It's my free period, and I want to change a few of my displays,' Miss Quinn explains, setting the fabric down on the tabletops. 'Get a bit of colour into the classroom. Thank you, Hannah!'

'No problem, Miss,' I grin, untangling myself from the Swiss cheese plant, which is trying to ruffle my hair with its fat, green fingers. 'See you later.'

The bell is ringing, but I push past the crowd of sleepy Monday-morning faces and nip into the girls' loos to fix my hair. I pick catkins from behind my ears and a wisp of hazel twig from my blazer. I brush my hair out and force my lips into a reluctant smile.

I've missed registration and I'm late for history, but I don't care enough to hurry. By the time I head out from the loos, the corridors are quiet.

As I approach the stairs, a small shower of coloured felt pens falls down the centre of the stairwell. A scattering of pencils and biros follows, and then a hail of squashed sandwiches, on granary bread. One catches me on the shoulder, and I pick it off gingerly. Cheese and pickle.

'Hey!' I shout up the stairs. 'Watch what you're doing!'

There's no reply, but half a dozen exercise books flutter down next, landing in a heap on the floor. I crane my neck to look up to the floors above, then duck out of the way as a huge chemistry textbook crashes down.

Someone is being hassled, their bag emptied out and flung down several flights of stairs. This is not good. I would like to turn away and ignore the sudden downpour, but my history class is in Room 31, at the top of this staircase.

I hesitate, then walk up the stairs, slowly, warily. On the second-floor landing, there's a knot of S2 boys. Paul stands in the corner, his face pale, unsmiling. Kenny Murphy, Fergus Brown and Tom Greenway stand on the stairs, laughing. Kenny's holding a glass bottle of Cherryade over the stairwell, while Tom dangles Paul's school bag, taunting.

These are Kit's friends, and they were Paul's friends too until a few weeks ago. Now they look anything but friendly.

'What's going on?' I demand.

'It's OK, Hannah,' Paul sighs. 'Just Kenny's idea of a joke.'

'Yeah, it's a real laugh,' I snap. 'Bunch of losers.'

'This is private, Hannah,' Kenny Murphy says. 'Run along to class, like a good little girl.'

I realize how much I dislike Kenny Murphy. His face is twisted into a tight, mean snarl of a smile.

'Don't tell *me* what to do,' I mutter, sounding braver than I feel. 'And leave Paul alone. He's my friend.'

'Oooh!' Fergus says in a mock-squeal. 'He's your friend, is he? Cute!'

'If you want your stuff, Muppet-boy, you just have to come and get it,' Kenny Murphy says. He waves the bottle of Cherryade about tauntingly.

'I don't want to fight,' Paul says coolly.

'No, girls don't fight, do they?' Kenny laughs. 'Oops! Dropped it . . .'

The bottle of Cherryade plummets down the stairwell and smashes into pieces at the bottom. A pool of red, sticky liquid seeps out over the fallen books and pencils, like someone's been shot.

Tom drops the dangling school bag after the rest, laughing.

'Nice talking to you, Hannah,' Kenny Murphy snaps. 'I'd choose my friends more carefully, though, if I were you. Your little boyfriend here . . . well, you can see what a loser he is.'

Kenny leans forward and flicks Paul's tie so that it slaps him in the face. Paul doesn't even flinch, just gazes out of the window as though he's a million miles away.

'See you around, Muppet,' Kenny says, then

turns away and saunters down the stairs, Tom and Fergus on his heels.

Paul takes a deep breath in. He pushes the hair back from his face with a shaky hand.

'Paul?'

'Don't, Hannah,' he says. 'I don't want to talk about it.'

'But you'll have to talk about it!' I exclaim. 'You'll have to tell Jed and Eva, and the teachers. This is bullying, Paul. Look what they did to your stuff!'

'It's OK,' Paul shrugs. 'It doesn't matter.'

I'm speechless.

'It does matter!' I protest. 'Paul, you can't ignore this!'

'Watch me,' he says. 'And if I can, you can. Stay out of this, Hannah. Please.'

He shoves past me, going down the stairs. I look down the stairwell and see him kneeling in the mess of glass and pop and crumpled books, mopping at things with a tissue and stuffing them back into his bag. I turn and climb the stairs to Room 31.

CHAPTER 12

You cannot let lads like Murphy, Tom and Fergus shove you around and call you names and trash your school stuff. If Paul ignores it, they'll know they can get away with it – he may as well scrawl *victim* on his forehead in thick black marker pen.

I spend all day worrying about Paul, and although I hang out in the art room all lunchtime, waiting for him, he doesn't show. Later, on the bus ride home, he tells me he walked down to the harbour to watch the fishing boats unload.

'I was worried,' I tell him. 'Y'know, after this morning . . .'

'Don't want to talk about it,' he says. 'It never happened.'

'But . . .'

'But nothing,' Paul says gently. 'I can handle this. Trust me. Stay out of it, and don't even think about telling Jed and Eva. Or the teachers. Promise?'

I don't want to promise. It feels like promising to stab your best mate in the back with a rusty compass point. Staying silent on this is a big mistake, I just know it.

'Hannah?' Paul asks. 'I'm asking you not to tell Jed and Eva, or the teachers. It'll just make everything a million times worse, OK? They'll tell my social workers, and then everything'll go pear-shaped. I like it here, Hannah. I want to stay.'

'I want you to stay as well,' I say.

'So promise.'

'I promise.'

'OK,' Paul grins, unwrapping a chocolate bar and handing me a square. 'It's sorted.'

I put the chocolate in my mouth, but it doesn't quite take away the bad taste that's there.

Later on, after tea, I knock at Kit's door as he's getting ready to go out. He's moulding his hair into pointy spikes with some kind of red hair gel that stains his fingers. He looks like he's just butchered a small animal and wiped the gore all over his head. Joey will be impressed.

'What d'*you* want?' he says, which is polite, for Kit.

'Nothing much,' I say.

'Push off then, I'm busy.'

I wander into the room and sit down on the midden that is Kit's bed. Paul made me promise not to tell Jed and Eva, or the teachers. He didn't mention Kit.

'Y'know Paul?' I begin.

'*That* muppet,' Kit scoffs. 'What's he done now?'

'It's not what Paul's done, it's what your so-called mates have done!' I explode. 'They're giving him loads of hassle at school. Picking on him, messing up his stuff and calling him names.'

Kit leans against the chest of drawers, wiping his hands on an old T-shirt.

'So he went running to you,' he says. 'Typical.'

'He did not,' I argue. 'He told me to stay out of it. But I can't, Kit. Murphy and Tom and Fergus really hate Paul Slater. I don't know why. He never did them any harm – I mean, they were all friends once, weren't they?'

Kit frowns. 'Not really,' he says. 'Paul's a weirdo, and they were pretty quick to catch on to that. Face it, Hannah, he doesn't even try.'

'He does!'

Kit shrugs, tugging at his flapping jeans so that exactly four centimetres of boxer shorts is visible above the belt. He looks like his jeans could fall down at any minute, but he's happy.

'Paul doesn't even mix much with the Donovans,' Kit argues. 'Heads off early to the pool most days to swim, hangs out at the beach all on his own, mopes around with that stupid sketchbook –'

'Kit, stop it!' I snap. 'You were there when Paul told us about his mum. You can't expect him to be a bundle of laughs, can you? What d'you think it feels like, being dragged around the countryside from one foster-family or children's home to another? What d'you think it feels like, knowing your mum left you? Not knowing if you'll ever see her again?'

'Maybe she had the right idea.'

'Kit, that's an awful thing to say!' I protest. 'Paul's being bullied. That's not right.'

Kit sighs. 'Hannah, don't hook up with this kid,' he tells me. 'He's trouble. If the lads are picking on him, it's because he's asking for it. Murphy, Tom and Fergus aren't exactly thugs, are they? They're not bullies.'

They looked like bullies this morning, tipping books and pencils and cheese-and-pickle sandwiches down the stairwell, but I don't say that. Kit doesn't want to know.

'It's just a bit of joking around,' Kit says. 'Paul's making too much of it. What a saddo.'

Some of the disappointment and disgust I'm feeling must leak out of my eyes, because Kit sits down on the bed and pinches my cheek. I smile sadly and remember the days when I thought my big brother was the coolest boy in the world. Not any more.

'Look, Hannah, I'll speak to the lads,' he says. 'Get them to back off a bit. OK?'

'Thanks, Kit,' I whisper. 'They're out of order, seriously.'

'Maybe.'

Kit checks his hair in the mirror, grabs a jacket and heads out of the door, on his way to another evening of hanging out by the chippy in Kirklaggan with Joey. He flicks off the light switch as he goes, leaving me alone in the dark.

Aliens came and took my brother, Kit, and swapped him for this vain, grumpy lookalike. The real Kit, the nice Kit, the one who once had a scrap with Murphy because he was pulling the legs off a spider, is probably stranded in cyberspace, eating vitamin pills, wearing a silver catsuit and having his brain scanned for signs of intelligence every few days. Maybe, while they were at it, the aliens took Joey too? It would explain a lot.

I drift over to the window, press my face against the cold glass. I am not in a sci-fi movie – this is real life. My best mate and my brother have deserted me for the Planet Slush, and nobody but me seems to care. If Krusty was here, curled up round my neck or slinking around my feet like a small, furry alarm clock, it wouldn't be so bad.

I pad back to my room, put on a Good Charlotte CD and dig out an old notebook. I fill two pages with sketches of a blissed-out, furry, bin-hopping kitten called Krusty before crashing out, fully clothed, on the rumpled quilt.

CHAPTER 13

Paul Slater gets on the school bus with two dinky little plaits tucked behind his ears. Even I do a double-take, and a bunch of S1 lads at the front of the bus erupts into snorts of disgust. There are a few catcalls from the back, but when I look round I see that Kit is trying to silence the hecklers. Trying, but not very hard.

'Hi, Hannah,' Paul grins, clattering into the seat across the aisle.

'What's he playing at?' I whisper as Joey flops down beside me. '*Plaits?* Tell me you didn't encourage him, Joey. This boy has enough problems already.'

Joey shrugs. 'Don't blame me,' she hisses. 'Why can't he have plaits? It's a statement, isn't it?'

Yup, it's a statement, all right. It might mean

take-me-as-I-am, in a cool, goth-guy kind of way. It might mean I-don't-care, forget-the-rules, I'm-not-like-you. Or it might mean pick-on-me cos I'm a wuss, a girly, a hippy-dippy gimp.

I think I know how Murphy and his mates will read it. They'll make mashed potato out of Paul Slater, probably before morning break. It's like sending a toddler to play in the traffic.

'We have to talk about Paul,' I say to Joey. 'He's a living, breathing disaster area. He needs our help.'

'You think?' Joey asks. Plaits on a boy are not a problem for her. Who knows, maybe even horns and a tail on a boy would be OK in her book.

'I think,' I say. 'Seriously. After hockey? Can you shake free of Kit for a while?'

'Guess so,' Joey shrugs. 'No problem.'

After hockey, when we're pink-faced and perspiring and our shins are black and blue from the assault of a dozen enemy hockey sticks, we trail back up the field, mud-spattered, mauled, but not defeated.

'How come boys don't play hockey?' I ask, my breath coming in ragged gasps. 'Why should we be the only ones to suffer?'

'Boys have no stamina,' Joey pronounces. 'They have to stick to lightweight games like footy. It's not their fault. Girls are the superior sex – we're brighter, cooler, smarter, stronger.'

A little coven of blonde gigglers from the enemy team glance back at Joey, rolling their eyes and nudging each other.

'What happened to your hair, Joey?' asks Karen McKay, the nastiest of the crew. 'An accident with the ketchup, was it? You're just so *cool*, Joey. I wish I had your style.'

Karen turns away, doubled up with laughter.

'OK, not every girl,' Joey admits. 'Karen didn't do so well with the *brighter, cooler, smarter* bit.'

'How about *blonder, meaner, dimmer*?' I suggest.

As we get up to the playground, the bell rings for break and a sea of kids spills out of the building.

'Hey, gorgeous!'

My brother is waving at Joey across the playground, blowing wolf whistles because she is just so irresistible when splattered with mud and dressed in a grey wraparound gymskirt.

Joey laughs, but Karen McKay seems to think the whistles are aimed at her, because she tosses her hair and sticks out her chest and starts wiggling her bum. Joey and I choke back the giggles as Karen flicks a little wave at Kit and his mates.

He's almost up level with us by now, and he casts a bemused glance at Karen as she licks her lips and flutters her eyelashes at him. She hitches her skirt a bit higher, displaying a few extra inches of orange, fake-tanned, goose-pimpled thigh. Attractive.

It happens so fast that even I don't catch on that it's Joey. I just see Karen hit the grass in a tangle of hockey sticks and legs and swearing. She's broken a nail and her knees are muddy and green, and she's screaming at Joey, calling her a stupid, clumsy, stripy-haired little cow.

'Hang on,' says Kit, 'watch what you're saying. It was an accident. You should have looked where you were going.'

'Yeah, you seemed a bit . . . preoccupied,' I point out.

Karen gets to her feet, brushing gobbets of mud off her skirt and scowling at Joey. 'You know what you did,' she hisses. 'And I'll get you for it, you sad little freak.'

Joey shrugs. 'Like Kit says, it was an accident, Karen,' she says, smirking. 'Sorry. I guess I'm not too good at keeping my hockey stick under control.'

That'll be why she just scored four goals in today's match, then.

'No hard feelings?' Joey asks, and then fakes surprise as Karen storms away, limping slightly.

I stare at Joey, eyes wide, and she shrugs and grins and winks when she thinks nobody's looking. You don't mess with Joey Donovan. I remember the Primary Two Christmas party when Santa handed her a pressie that turned out to be a big box of Liquorice Allsorts. She marched back up to Santa and demanded a swap.

'You made a mistake,' she told him bluntly. 'You know I don't like Liquorice Allsorts. I want chocolate truffles, like Hannah, or I'm not going to believe in you any more.'

She stared very hard at Santa, who was really Mr Gillespie, the janitor, until he coughed up with the last box of chocolate truffles. He was scared of her for years afterwards.

'I'll wait for you by the tennis courts,' Kit says to Joey now. 'Hurry up. And watch what you're doing with that hockey stick!'

Joey hooks Kit round the neck with her stick, drops a little kiss on the end of his nose, then turns away.

'I'm busy this breaktime,' she says. 'Girl stuff. I'll catch you at lunchtime, maybe?'

'If *I'm* not busy,' Kit shoots back. 'Hey, if you see Karen McKay, tell her I'm down by the tennis courts . . .'

'Don't even think about it,' Joey says sweetly. 'I have a ruthless side, y'know.'

We run up to the changing rooms and grab a shower before the water runs cold, then get dressed quickly. Karen McKay hangs about for ages by the mirror, applying mascara and sparkly lipgloss while her friends fuss with their hair.

They sweep out of the changing rooms together. 'Saddo,' Karen whispers as she goes, and Joey gives her the finger behind her back before moving up to the mirror to slick on black lippy and eyeliner.

'I'll break both her legs next time if she tries that flirty stuff with Kit again,' Joey sniffs. 'Do you think it was Karen who sent Kit the valentine? She doesn't care whose boyfriend she goes for.'

'A KitKat and a tattoo?' I say. 'Not her style. Not that she's got a style, exactly.'

'Tell me about it,' Joey laughs. 'As if he'd be interested in an airhead like that.'

'As if,' I echo, but with less conviction. Joey Donovan happens to be just about the smartest girl in S1, but she's not smart enough to notice that lads very rarely pick out girlfriends for their IQ.

'Anyway,' says Joey, 'you wanted to talk about Paul.'

'Yeah,' I say. 'He's in big trouble, Joey. He needs our help.'

But before we get any further, the bell rings out to signal the end of break, and Joey rolls her eyes. 'Breaktimes are getting shorter, I swear,' she huffs. 'We'll meet up at lunchtime, OK?'

'Suppose so,' I agree, but I can't help wondering if Paul Slater will be mince and tatties by then, plaits or no plaits.

CHAPTER 14

At lunchtime, we hide out in the French classroom. Joey, who always gets top marks for French, volunteers to clear away the textbooks and collect in the worksheets. 'Close the classroom door on your way out,' Mr Marlow says.

'We will,' Joey says sweetly. She forgets to mention that we won't be leaving till lunchtime is over, but then again, Mr Marlow doesn't ask.

I munch on a sad cheese triangle and a bunch of Ritz crackers, while Joey gets stuck into some kind of wholemeal quiche with rocket and cherry-tomato salad. 'So?' she says.

'So. Paul is being bullied,' I tell her. 'Kenny Murphy and Fergus Brown and Tom Greenway. They're trashing his stuff, pushing him about, calling him names. I saw them yesterday, and it's serious stuff, but Paul won't speak out.'

'Are you sure about this?' Joey asks. 'Murphy, Fergus and Tom aren't bullies, are they? They're OK. They're popular. They don't need to push anyone around. Maybe you got it wrong?'

'Joey, I didn't get it wrong. They're making Paul's life a misery.'

'The best way to deal with bullying is to blank it,' Joey says. 'That's what I do. You pretend you don't care, act like you couldn't give a stuff. Most bullies will get bored and give up.'

I know that this tactic works for Joey, but she's a tough cookie. Anyone who really tangles with her is asking for trouble, as Karen McKay discovered. I'm not sure if Paul has that same streak.

'Paul *has* been ignoring it,' I explain, 'but it's just getting worse.'

We're sitting by the window, and looking down we can see the playground spread out below us. Murphy, Fergus, Tom and Kit are playing footy with a gang of other S2 lads. Paul walks past them, at a safe distance, eating chips from crumpled paper. He's still in one piece, in spite of the plaits.

As we watch, though, the football slams into him, hard, scattering chips across the playground.

'That was probably an accident,' Joey says quickly.

'It probably wasn't,' I correct her. 'Come on, Joey. Don't kid yourself.'

I look to see whether Kit is saying anything to Murphy and the lads, but I can't tell. If he has told them to back off, it's not exactly obvious.

'Maybe he should just stay in the art room,' Joey says.

'Yeah, right!' I protest. 'He can't stay holed up forever! He has to go to lessons; he has to see these losers in the playground, in the corridors, on the footy field. He has to find a way to handle it, and plaits aren't the way I'd have picked. It's kind of like *asking* for trouble.'

Joey frowns. 'Look, if Murphy and his crew are hassling Paul, it's not because of the plaits, is it?' she points out. 'They were doing it before. He's just – well, different, isn't he? He doesn't care about fitting in. Why shouldn't he look the way he wants? Stand out from the crowd, be individual?'

Joey has a point. Paul is getting bullied anyhow, so maybe the plaits won't make any difference.

'He's a big boy, Hannah. He makes his own choices,' Joey says. 'We're all in charge of our own lives, aren't we?'

Maybe. But Paul didn't choose for his mum to disappear, to be taken into care, and yet it seems like he's stuck with it.

'People just don't like him,' I say. 'Kit doesn't,

Murphy doesn't. I don't get it – he seems OK to me. He's thoughtful. He's kind. What's not to like?'

'It's not that simple,' Joey shrugs. 'Paul is great – you know that and I know that – but he's complicated. Messed up too. People pick up on that. He spooks them out, like with Kit that time. How weird was that?'

'Weird,' I admit.

Joey bites into a slice of Eva's carrot cake, brushing the crumbs from her frayed black skirt.

'We're his mates,' she announces. 'You and me and Kit. Well, you and me, anyway. We can look out for him, but we can't change him. If he wants to have plaits, maybe that's a good thing. Better than trying to be like everyone else and ending up different anyway.'

'Maybe.'

Joey looks out of the window again, her gaze following Kit as he sprints around the playground in pursuit of a football. Her eyes go all soft and mushy. 'Am I being a rubbish mate just now?' she asks me.

'Totally rubbish. Hopeless.'

She laughs. 'OK, you can lie a little bit, y'know, to save my feelings.'

'You're not so bad,' I admit. 'It's awkward, because it's Kit, but I'm trying to understand. I guess I never imagined we'd get tangled up with lads just yet. I didn't expect it.'

'I decided to get it out of the way now,' Joey says. 'Dating and stuff. Later on, I'll be busy with Standard Grades and Highers and university, and I won't have time for boys.'

'D'you think it works like that?' I ask, amazed.

'It's an experiment,' Joey says. 'So far, I like it. But I could give it up any time I like.'

'That's what Kenny Murphy says about smoking,' I point out.

At this moment, Mr Marlow comes into the classroom with a mug of coffee and a large Danish pastry.

'Girls, what are you still doing here?' he barks gruffly.

'Tidying up, sir,' Joey says sweetly. 'There was a terrible mess round Karen McKay's desk. Sweet wrappers, old chewing gum, used tissues, false fingernails. Yeuww. We've cleared it all up, though, as you can see.'

Mr Marlow looks doubtful, but he says nothing as Joey and I leave the classroom, dropping our lunch wrappers in the bin as we pass.

'You're a terrible liar,' I whisper to Joey as we go.

'I know,' she grins. 'But, hey, I could give it up any time I like . . .'

CHAPTER 15

This is a seriously bad idea.

It's Saturday morning and I sit on the washing basket in the bathroom at Beachcomber Cottage, trying to distance myself from the whole thing. Krusty is batting the lid of the dye bottle around the bathroom floor, getting under everyone's feet, while Itchy and Scratchy are curled up among the towels on the shelf, purring.

'Is it working?' asks Paul, his head over the sink. Drips of thick green sludge snake down his neck and plop on to the floorboards beneath. One lands on Krusty, and I wipe it off quickly before she ends up with emerald polka dots.

'Of course it's working,' Joey scoffs. 'I'm an expert, aren't I? You're in safe hands.'

One safe hand, encased in a pink rubber glove, grips Paul firmly round the neck while the other directs the shower head at his scalp. He wriggles and yelps.

'It's too hot!' he protests. 'You'll burn me!'

'Don't be such a wimp,' scolds Joey. 'Stay still. We have to rinse until the water runs clear. Or until you faint, whichever is sooner.'

She adjusts the water temperature and Paul survives until the water runs clear.

'Better change your top,' Joey says, noting the big water stains on Paul's long-sleeved T-shirt. 'It's soaking.'

'Nah, it'll soon dry,' Paul shrugs, tugging the sleeves down so they cover his hands. It's a habit he has, something he does when he's nervous. We troop through to Joey's room to finish off with the hairdryer. Paul's hair is very, very green.

'Excellent,' Joey says. 'That'll make 'em sit up and take notice.'

'And that's what you want, is it?' I ask.

'Doesn't matter what they think,' Paul says. '*I* like it. C'mon, Hannah, it's cool, admit it.'

Paul makes two green plaits to hang down either side of his face, then pulls the rest of his hair back in a scruffy ponytail. I liked it better when it was toffee-coloured and loose, but I don't say so. Paul is playing with the eyeliners and shaders on Joey's dressing table.

'How do girls do all this stuff?' he asks idly. 'I've always wondered. I bet you need a steady hand. Think I need a more dramatic look to go with the green?'

'No,' I snap. 'It's girly enough already. Murphy's lot will have a field day with this, you know they will.'

Paul puts down the eyeliner and pulls a face. 'I can't be a mouse all my life just in case I upset that loser,' he says.

'No way,' Joey says. 'Show 'em you don't give a stuff. Let's see what Jed and Eva think, yeah?'

Downstairs, Jed and Eva are making a driftwood mirror on the kitchen table. Jed arranges the bits of wood and glue-guns them into place, and Eva adds spirals of frayed rope, seashells and seaglass. If they're surprised by Paul's hair, they don't show it. After Joey's experiments, they are probably shockproof.

'Good colour,' Eva comments. 'Very vivid.'

'It lasts for ten to fifteen washes,' I say anxiously.

'Great,' Eva grins.

'You look like a freak,' Mikey says, looking up from his toy cars in the corner. 'Why d'you want hair like seaweed?'

'It's cool,' says Joey. 'He doesn't look like a freak – he looks like a goth.'

'Well, *I* think he looks like a freak.'

That's what Kit thinks too when he turns up later to hang out with Joey. His eyebrows shoot up about an inch and he mimes sticking a finger down his throat when Joey and Paul aren't looking.

'Sheesh kebab,' he says carefully. 'Interesting look, Paul. Very . . . *unusual.*'

'I like it,' Paul says.

'That's OK, then,' Kit shrugs. 'I reckon Murphy will, as well.'

'That's his problem,' Paul says.

But all of us know that if Murphy has a problem, Paul has too.

Kit and Joey retreat to the bin-bag cavern to listen to clashy, trashy music.

'Coming down to the beach?' Paul asks. 'Let Krusty play in the surf?'

We trail down to the water's edge, Krusty skittering on ahead. She thinks she is a dog, not a small tortoiseshell kitten. Her tail swishes from side to side and she chases every bit of windblown seaweed, every fleck of surf. She stalks seagulls, sniffs the breeze.

The water is a wide, shimmering stripe of silver hung beneath a steel-grey sky, with Seal Island just out of reach in the bay.

'D'you ever go out to the island?' Paul asks. 'It looks kind of magical, sitting there. Perfect.'

'I know what you mean,' I tell him. 'We camped there once, Joey and me – on one of the beaches. We couldn't get to sleep with the sound of the waves crashing all around us and the screeching of the gulls overhead, so we sat up all night and told ghost stories and scared ourselves stupid.'

'Spooky,' says Paul. 'Maybe it wasn't the waves or the gulls, though. It might have been the seal people, shrugging off their skins and dancing on the beach in the moonlight.'

'What?'

'Well, you know,' Paul teases. 'Some people say that seals are the spirits of people who drown at sea, and that they can cast off their skins and take on human form again in the moonlight . . .'

'I'm glad we didn't know *that* back then!' I laugh, but I can't quite shake off the shivery feeling that Paul's story has given me.

'How did you get there?' he asks. 'Can you swim?'

'No way,' I tell him. 'It's too far, and there are currents. No, Jed used to row us out. He's got an old dinghy.'

'Seal Island,' Paul says softly. 'It's like the land beyond the sea.'

'Nah, just a lump of rock with wraparound

beaches and scrubby grass – nothing much to do, unless you're a seal or a cormorant.'

'Doesn't matter,' Paul shrugs. 'Islands are magic. Special.'

Paul stands for a long time looking out towards Seal Island, and I wonder if he's thinking about the days when he lived on Mull. Was that special and magical too? Or did it just seem that way, because he had a mum and a home and a cat called Splodge?

Paul frowns suddenly, picking up some stones to skim. I join in.

'Be cool if the beach magic really worked,' I say to Paul. 'Y'know, the tide wishes, the skimming stones.'

'It does,' Paul says seriously. 'Murphy's lot have been less full-on lately. And Kit's been almost friendly.'

'Don't get your hopes up.'

'No. No, I won't,' Paul says. 'I've learned that lesson the hard way.'

He looks so sad that I want to take his hand and squeeze it tight, stroke his stupid green hair and touch the pale skin of his cheek. I don't, of course.

Paul picks up a clump of shrivelled seaweed and starts to drag it about the beach for Krusty to chase. She hunts and pounces, leaps and rolls and zigzags into the surf. When she gets wet, she just shakes herself and carries on, a small, bedraggled bundle of energy.

Paul crouches down to stroke her. 'Crazy cat,' he laughs. 'Didn't anyone tell you you're meant to hate water? Didn't anyone tell you how to be a cat?'

'She's the best cat in the world,' I argue, bursting with pride.

'She's nuts. Haven't managed to talk your mum round about keeping her, then?'

'No chance,' I tell him. 'Mum thinks cats are trouble, all fleas and scratched furniture and stinky litter trays. Maybe Krusty should be your cat?' It hurts me to say it, but if anyone else is going to look after Krusty, I'd want it to be Paul.

'I'd like to, Hannah,' he says. 'But you can't just decide who owns a cat, didn't you know that? It's the other way round. Cats choose *you*. And Krusty picked you out, way back, right about when you picked her out of the dustbin, I guess. You're stuck with each other.'

'That's OK by me,' I grin.

'Cool. I'm here if you need backup, anyhow. Green-haired misfit, good at opening tins, needs all the friends he can get.'

'I'm your friend,' I say.

'I know you are, Hannah,' says Paul. 'I know.'

OK, this should be the moment where he reaches over and kisses me, or looks into my eyes, or pulls me close and hugs me while the breeze whips our hair into a tangle and lashes our faces with saltwater and sand. It's not happening. Instead, Paul grabs up the clump of seaweed and sprints off along the beach, Krusty in hot pursuit.

I watch him go. A hundred metres away, he leaps in the air, hurdling a big driftwood branch, and something small and black drops out of his coat pocket and flaps down on to the sand. I scuff along the tideline, picking up shells. Beside the driftwood branch, I see a black sketchbook on the sand, pages fluttering.

I pick it up, flick through, scanning page after page of cartoon figures in what looks like a comic-book story. There are three superheroes with cat faces, slanting catlike eyes and pointed ears peeking out through their hair. One of the cat characters looks very like Kit, with a wide grin and dark, spiky hair. Another has stripy hair in mussed-up plaits, just like Joey. The third cat character is small and cute and kittenish, with a blunt-cut bob and hairclips just like mine.

What is it with little cartoon cat faces? They remind me of Kit's valentine tattoo, but I push the thought away. Paul wouldn't send a tattoo to my brother. Would he?

'Did I drop it?' Paul is right behind me, taking the book out of my hands gently, folding it shut.

'I just noticed it on the sand . . .' I say, but Paul has stuffed the book back into his parka pocket and is already walking away. 'It looks brilliant,' I tell him. 'Maybe I could read it sometime?'

'When it's finished, maybe,' Paul says into the wind.

'I'd like that.'

We collect armfuls of driftwood and pocketfuls of shells, and scratch wishes into the sand with a driftwood stick for the tide to take before heading up to Beachcomber Cottage. Krusty sits on my shoulder, her tail swishing the whole way back.

CHAPTER 16

Mr McKenzie is not pleased. He pulls Paul out of lessons on Monday morning and hauls Jed and Eva in for an emergency meeting. He is holding them directly responsible for the green hair. After all, they have already parented one social misfit (Joey) who is incapable of sticking to the school uniform code. Paul is clearly being led astray.

Paul explains all this in the art room at lunchtime, between sips of Cherryade.

'Mr McKenzie is not a happy man,' Paul is saying. 'He told Jed and Eva to get my hair dyed back to brown, so Jed asked if all dyed hair is against the school rules, and McKenzie said it definitely was. Jed said that in that case they can't possibly dye my hair back to brown, we'll just have to wait for it to fade out. McKenzie looked like he might explode. Seriously.'

'So you get to keep your hair green?'

'Yup. For now. McKenzie says there'll be a new school uniform letter going out after the Easter holidays.'

I shake my head. 'You got away with it!'

'Maybe,' Paul grins, 'but McKenzie is on my case, and Joey had better watch out too. Apparently, green hair is just one step away from drugged-up, child-eating terrorist.'

'Understandable,' I say. 'This is a man who thinks that minikilts threaten the fabric of society. Sad.'

Paul takes out his folder, slides his painting on to the desktop. He studies it, frowning. It's finished now – Paul has spent plenty of lunchtimes in the art room this term. I should know. I have too.

'Like the hair, Paul,' Miss Quinn says, coming over. 'Mr McKenzie doesn't, though. We've been hearing all about it in the staffroom.'

'I bet,' Paul grins.

She turns her attention to the painting. 'Finished, then? You've got something here. Real feeling. Pleased?'

'Dunno,' Paul admits. 'Something's not working, but I don't know which bit. Is it the expressions? The light and dark?'

Miss Quinn peers more closely. 'Could be a bit

of both. Did you work from a photo, Paul?'

'Just from my head.'

'That's it, then,' she says. 'It's powerful, but you just didn't have all the information you needed. Next time, work from life. The model's there right in front of you. There's a portrait competition coming up – why not have a go?'

Paul shrugs.

'Hannah could model,' Miss Quinn says thoughtfully.

'Bad idea,' I say, rolling my eyes. 'You don't want to be stuck painting *me*.'

'Don't I?'

Two spots of colour flare in my cheeks, but Miss Quinn just smiles and wanders off, sipping her coffee.

'I'd be a terrible model,' I protest. 'The invisible girl.'

'Not to me.'

Paul gets a drawing board and some big sheets of paper, and I sit back in my chair, one hand fiddling anxiously with the neck of my school sweatshirt. When I steal a glance at Paul, he's looking right at me, eyes narrowed with concentration. I stop fiddling, suddenly paralysed, fixing my eyes on the wall behind Paul.

Why would anyone want to draw me? I may not be invisible, but I am a girl who plays it safe. I am never likely to dye my hair crazy colours or wear stripy tights and chopped-up shirts to school. I don't come top of the class for anything, or bottom of the class, either. I blend in, like a patched bit of wallpaper. Paul looks at me and sees the outside stuff – does he think that's all there is?

Across the table, his rucksack lies open, a heap of books spilling out. One of them is the little black sketchbook full of comic-book characters that dropped on to the sand at the weekend. I remember that Paul doesn't see anything the way it seems. He has a different slant. To him, I am a wide-eyed cat-girl with twitching whiskers.

'Miaow,' I say.

He looks up, grinning. 'Miaow, yourself,' he replies. 'And no, Hannah, you can't see my sketchbook. Not yet.'

'But I'm in it!'

'No,' Paul corrects. 'You're not in it. KittenKat is.'

'KittenKat?'

'That's all I'm saying.'

'Don't want to read it anyway,' I huff.

'No, I can see that! Stop moving, will you?'

I find a patch of blue sky outside the art-room window and focus my attention on it. A lone seagull flies past, but otherwise that patch of blue is pretty unexciting.

'McKenzie really is a maniac,' Paul says after a

while. 'I mean, there are kids in this school who bully, kids who smoke, kids who drink or steal or beat each other up for a laugh. Trouble is, all that stuff is too tough to prove. Easier to pick on the kid with the funny hair.'

'He was never going to *like* it,' I point out.

'Kenny Murphy dyes his hair,' Paul says thoughtfully.

He's right – Murphy has that carefully streaked kind of look where the tips of his hair are blond, the roots brown. It's the kind of look that requires a hairdresser, not a bottle of cheap hair dye and an old towel in the bathroom.

'Blond doesn't count,' I decide. 'Blond stands for young, clean, cool. It goes with shiny shoes and suntans and neatly pressed white shirts. No, it's green you have to watch out for – and pink, purple, red, blue, orange. Dangerous, dodgy.'

Paul peers over his drawing board, grinning. 'My days may be numbered with green,' he says, 'but there's a whole rainbow of possibilities out there . . .'

I shake my head sadly. For some people, there is just no hope.

CHAPTER 17

It's funny how you can get used to green hair, like you can get used to the idea of a cat who thinks she's a dog or a best friend who thinks she's in love with your brother.

By the time we break up for Easter, I'm so used to Paul's hair it seems like he's looked that way forever. I don't know how things are going with the bullying, but two weeks' break from snotty comments and having a football kicked at you every time you pass has got to be a good thing.

School holidays are a lovely, drifty time of sleep-ins and kids' TV and lazing around in pyjamas with our favourite CDs playing full blast. Mum and Dad are working, and now that Kit and I are both in high school they don't bother with babysitters or kids' clubs. That's OK. Nobody can tell me off for eating toast and jam for lunch or watching too much *Simpsons*, and as long as the house is tidy and the washing up's done by the time they get home, they don't get stressy.

Today, Kit headed off early with Joey and Eva. Eva is delivering driftwood mirrors, wind chimes and rope-handled treasure boxes to posh craft shops all around the Lake District. She agrees to drop Kit and Joey in Carlisle, then pick them up on the way back through.

It's the kind of day out I used to love, except that Joey and I never bailed out to the nearest city – we'd stick with Eva and help deliver the driftwood creations, wrapped in white tissue paper, to funny little shops in faraway towns and villages. We'd take one of Eva's fantastic picnics and stop to eat on the shores of Lake Windermere, or at a waterfall, a park, once even a rocky beach on the Isle of Arran where the sun set in streaks of red and pink. Good times.

Today, of course, I've been replaced. I flick through the cartoon channels, munching popcorn, refusing to let it get to me.

When the doorbell rings, I expect it to be the postman or the window cleaner, or maybe Murphy or Tom calling for Kit. Instead, there's Paul, green-haired and grinning on the garden path, his eyes ringed with eyeliner like a panda, a single black crow's feather hanging from one plait.

I decide not to mention it.

He is standing astride the weirdest bike I've ever seen in my life. The wheels seem to be slightly different sizes, the huge frame is painted in pink-and-turquoise zebra stripes, and there's a lidded basket in front of the handlebars that looks like something my granny might use to stash away her knitting wool and treacle toffee.

'Paul! What *is* that thing?' I ask. I'm grinning all over my face.

'Been making it out of old parts that Jed found. D'you like it?'

'Um . . . it's very unusual!' I bluff.

'Don't knock it,' says Paul. 'It's transport! With this little cutie we can go just about anywhere we like . . .'

'We?'

'Yes, *we*,' Paul grins. He unbuckles the basket lid and lifts it gently, and there's Krusty, peering out, her green eyes glinting.

I squeal and grab her, letting her squirm up into her favourite position round my neck, and Paul lets the bike clatter down on the pathway and we go inside. I pour apple juice for Paul and a saucer of milk for Krusty, who laps politely, as though she comes visiting every day.

'You're really here,' I tell her softly. 'This is *my* house. Maybe yours too, one day, if I manage to bribe my mum. What do you think?'

'Very nice,' Paul says, sipping apple juice.

'Not you,' I scold him. 'Look, Paul, she likes it. She's very well-behaved. If my mum could just see her, see how good she is . . .'

'She'd have a fit,' Paul says, and I know he's right. Not fair.

Krusty completes her exploration of the living room, climbs up my body and burrows in round my neck again. I lean back, loving the feel of warm fur against my skin, the flick of her tail across my throat.

'If beach magic works, how come my mum is still dead against Krusty?' I ask later, following Paul outside on to the path. 'It's not a big thing to ask.'

'Big thing, small thing, it doesn't matter,' he says. 'It works. You just have to be patient. Stuff doesn't always happen the way you expect it to.'

He hauls the bike upright and opens the basket to put Krusty inside. She turns in a circle several times, then settles down on the fold of cloth inside. Paul fastens the lid.

'Come on, then, Hannah,' he grins, pinging the bicycle bell a couple of times. 'Let's go to the beach!'

'Yeah, right!' I laugh. 'I'm not going anywhere on that old wreck!'

'Got something better to do?'

'No, but . . .'

'But what? We'll go to the beach, then back to the cottage. Eva left an apple pie,' Paul teases, and I'm done for, because there is no contest between supermarket popcorn and Eva's home-made apple pie.

Paul stands astride the zebra-striped bike, and I sit gingerly on the saddle, bright pink and terrified because I've never been this close to him before.

'C'mon, then!' he says, exasperated, grabbing my arms and hauling them round his waist. 'Let's go!' We bump off the kerb on to the lane, Paul standing up on the pedals, me leaning back on the saddle, petrified.

'No-ooo!' I shriek, but Paul just laughs.

We fly past a group of little kids kicking a ball about down by the church, and they laugh and point. Boy with plaits, green hair and panda eyes, me hanging on for dear life with my legs sticking out straight. I'd laugh too. I stick my tongue out at them and we whoosh past, and my hair lifts in the breeze and flies out behind me.

At the top of the lane, we see Murphy, Fergus and Tom on bikes. Fergus and Tom pedal off into the distance, but Murphy skids his BMX in front of us, and we swerve off the road and into a ditch.

'Idiot!' I snap at him. 'What d'you think you're doing?'

Murphy raises one eyebrow, watching us clamber out of the ditch.

'You're looking very *cute* today, Slater,' he says with a sly grin. 'Been trying out your girlfriend's make-up? Sweet.'

Paul frowns and huffs and turns away, but his cheeks flush pink.

Murphy smirks. 'Don't want to worry you, but I think a ratty old crow just died in your hair.'

I wait for Paul to answer back, but instead I can feel him curling up inside himself, cringing, cowering. His shoulders slump and he tugs down the sleeves of his jumper and stares at his scuffed-up baseball boots like they're the most fascinating things he ever saw.

'Get lost, Murphy,' I say, but it sounds feeble, even to me.

'Don't worry, Hannah, I'm going,' Murphy grins. He leans over to Paul and tugs on one green plait, his voice low and menacing. 'Don't try this look at school, Muppet. Seriously. I've been very patient, but you're starting to bug me.' Then he cycles away, whistling.

'Is Krusty OK?' I ask, sneaking a look in the basket.

'Think so.'

'You have to stand up to him,' I whisper.

'Not so easy,' Paul says. 'I can't. You know why.

If the social workers find out there's a problem, they'll pull the plug on this foster placement and drag me back to Glasgow like they have every other time, and I really don't want that to happen, Hannah. Let's just leave it, OK?'

So we do.

At the beach, Paul finds a couple of magic stones, chucks his worries out to sea. Krusty chases along the surf while Paul sticks a couple of gull feathers in the sand with a circle of seashells round them. He makes a star shape from tiny bits of driftwood with nuggets of seaglass in the middle, and a spiral from shells and tiny white pebbles.

'More beach magic?' I ask.

Paul nods. 'The feathers represent travel and freedom,' he says. 'The shells represent home, family. The stones are strength. The seaglass is love, beauty, art.'

I know he's making it up as he goes along, but it sounds cool, convincing.

'What about the driftwood?' I ask.

'The driftwood?' Paul repeats dreamily. 'That's me.'

'No,' I protest, but he just smiles, turning a smooth, pale branch of twisted wood round and round in his hands.

'The sea smoothes away all the rough edges,' Paul says softly. 'But it bleaches out the colour, the life, as well. Driftwood is different from other kinds of wood.'

'It's beautiful,' I say.

'Sometimes,' Paul agrees. 'Sometimes it can be salvaged, made into something useful or good, like Jed does. Other times, it can't. It goes back to the sea.'

Later that week, Paul and I are sharing a milkshake at the cafe in Kirklaggan when Karen McKay and her mates come in. They are loud and giggly and draped in Kirklaggan High footy scarves, squashing into the window seats and ordering cappuccinos.

I remember that today was the regional final of the school footy tournament. Kit has been playing and Joey has been watching, and Karen and her crew have clearly been watching too. Judging by the mood they're in, it looks like Kirklaggan have won.

'What was the score?' I call over, and Karen turns and looks at me like I'm some especially unpleasant kind of insect.

'Three–one to us,' she says grudgingly. 'Kit scored the last goal.'

'Cool,' I say.

Karen turns her gaze to Paul, taking in the panda eyes and the black crow's feather that seem to have become permanent features. She stifles a smirk.

'Don't you know anyone *normal*, Hannah?' she calls over.

'What, like you?' I ask. 'No. Lucky me.'

It's a question I've asked myself, though.

We get up and leave, making out like we planned it that way all along.

CHAPTER 18

McKenzie kicks off the new term with a whole-school assembly aimed at stamping out green hair, panda eyes and any last shreds of creativity and daring. He hands out a copy of the new, revised school uniform code, with added clauses that outlaw dyed hair, make-up and plaits on boys.

'He's losing it,' Joey whispers, peering up at McKenzie as he stalks across the stage. 'He can't enforce this. Half the girls wear make-up and plenty of them dye their hair too. As for the plaits thing, it's downright sexist. You can't just say that girls are allowed long hair and plaits and boys aren't – it's probably illegal.'

'It also says that frayed skirts, fishnets, striped socks and platform soles are not allowed,' I point out.

'Yeah, but they're like, *so* last month,' Joey whispers. 'It doesn't say anything about bin-bag minis.' She does a little shimmy so that her home-made skirt, constructed from a black garden-refuse sack, flutters out. The biker boots have been replaced with neon-pink jelly-shoes, and the plain black tights are tastefully laddered and torn.

This is a battle Joey will always win. McKenzie doesn't stand a chance.

'To enforce the new rules,' McKenzie booms out, 'I will need the support and cooperation of every pupil here. Kirklaggan High is a fine school, and I will not stand by and let it become a laughing stock. Certain elements here believe they can flout the rules and make a mockery of our school uniform, all in the name of individuality. Well, let me tell you, boys and girls, school is *not* about individuality. It is about teamwork, pulling together, standing firm against those who would like to see authority overthrown!'

'See?' Joey hisses. 'Lost it. Totally.'

A posse of S2 lads troops up on to the stage, including Murphy, Fergus, Tom and Kit. It's the footy squad, fresh from their success in the regional high school finals. They all look very smart and wholesome. Kit must have borrowed a school blazer, as he swapped his own for a Blink 182 CD sometime last year. As McKenzie presents the captain of the team with a shining silver trophy, he seems not to notice Murphy's expensively highlighted hair.

'These are lads we can be proud of,' McKenzie booms. 'Smart, sporting, successful – a credit to the school!'

Everyone cheers as Murphy holds the silver trophy high above his head. McKenzie, beaming with pride, shakes hands with each boy in the team, and the cheering reaches fever pitch. Even Joey is clapping.

'Just for Kit,' she whispers.

As we file out of the hall, I catch sight of Paul, shuffling along with the other S2s. He is wearing perfect uniform, just about, apart from the sweatbands on his wrists and the baseball boots and the way his shirt sleeves hang down over his hands. It's just his hair and his panda eyes that are such a threat to the school.

As I watch, he trips and stumbles, and the boys around him laugh. He stumbles again, and I wonder why none of the teachers can see what's happening. Because it *is* happening. The bullying has started again.

'You think he'd do something to tone down his hair,' says Kit, who hasn't repeated the experiment with the blood-red hair gel because it left a pink tidemark round his ears. 'And the make-up. Every morning, McKenzie makes him scrub it off. Why can't he learn? Is he stupid, or what?'

'Stubborn,' I say.

'Stupid,' says Kit.

We're on the school bus, sitting across the aisle from each other, bowling along towards Paul and Joey's stop.

'Tell your friends to lay off the bullying, Kit. He doesn't deserve it. They'll listen to you.'

'They won't,' Kit says. 'He's asking for it, isn't he? He should stop pushing the rules, keep his head down.'

'Would they like him, then?' I ask.

'Hannah, they'll never like him.'

The bus shudders to a halt and Paul and Joey get on. Joey sits next to Kit and Paul sits next to me. He has orange and black eyeshadow today, and what look like a couple of pheasant feathers in his hair.

'Chicken feathers?' Kit asks, and starts making clucking sounds until Joey tells him to shut up. I can't rely on my brother for help. He's starting to be part of the problem.

'Won't see you at lunch,' Paul says softly. 'Detention again. Sorry.'

'McKenzie is useless,' I say. 'Why don't you tell him what's going on? Or tell Jed and Eva.'

'No.'

'You can't just let them make your life a misery!' I protest.

We hang back and get off the bus last, but it doesn't make any difference, because Murphy is waiting for us on the pavement, chewing bubblegum. He blows a huge bubble, then takes the sickly pink gum out of his mouth, stretching it between his fingers.

'Hey, Muppet!' he shouts. 'I thought I told you to shove off back to Glasgow? Loser. Gay-boy.'

Paul puts his hands in his pockets and turns his face away. A pink, bubblegum missile scores a direct hit into his hair, but Paul seems barely to notice. We walk along in silence, skirting the school grounds and going in through the teachers' car park to avoid McKenzie.

'Why d'you let him get away with it?' I explode suddenly, when we reach the quiet and shelter of the kitchen bins. 'How can you *stand* it?'

I reach up to drag the sticky pink gum out of Paul's hair, but it's just a tangle of green hair and gunk and feathers. The gum smells sweet, but it disgusts me. It's been in Murphy's mouth.

'Doesn't matter,' Paul says dully.

'It does!' I rage. 'Paul, I can't get this out. We'll need to find some scissors.'

'Use this.' Paul takes a flick knife from his pocket and opens the blade. He tests it with his fingertip, drawing a bright bead of blood.

'What are you doing with a knife?' I say, horrified. 'The hair and the make-up, that's one thing, but this . . . you could hurt somebody!'

Paul looks at me with soft panda eyes and gently shakes his head. 'Hannah, you know I'd never do that.'

'No, but if McKenzie found out . . .'

'He won't, will he?'

I take the knife gingerly and slice the bubblegum from Paul's hair, letting it fall on to the concrete below. His hair looks kind of hacked about, but at least the pink mess has gone.

'You shouldn't let him call you those things,' I say sadly. 'Don't you hate it? Doesn't it hurt you?'

Paul shrugs and rearranges the pheasant feathers.

'He called you *loser*,' I say disgustedly. 'He called you *gay*.'

Paul trails a finger along my lip, nudging it into a smile. He tilts my chin up, makes me look right into his sea-green eyes. My lips tremble, and my heart begins to race.

'It doesn't matter,' Paul repeats. 'Hannah, don't worry about me. It really doesn't matter what Murphy thinks.'

Then he smiles and shrugs and slowly walks away.

CHAPTER 19

Paul is in trouble. I don't know how many times a day Murphy and his crew call him names, push him, shove him or kick him, but I know it's plenty. I can see him pulling back, building a wall round himself, a shell. The hair and the feathers and the panda eyes are just a part of it.

Don't touch, the shell says. I'm tough, I'm strong, back off.

It isn't working. Murphy and his mates look clean and smart and wholesome, but they are the kind of kids who stomp through rock pools in their wellies, smashing shells, pulling the legs off crabs while the grown-ups look on fondly.

Every lunchtime, Paul is in detention. Joey is usually with Kit, so I hang out on my own in the art room, picking at my lunch and washing palettes for Miss Quinn.

'Just you again today, Hannah?' she asks. 'What's happened to Paul? I was hoping he'd get to finish that portrait of you before the competition closing date. I'd love to put it forward.'

'Paul's in trouble with Mr McKenzie,' I tell her. 'He's getting detention the whole time because of the hair, the feathers, the black eyeliner. Mr McKenzie's trying to wear him down, but Paul won't give up.'

'Ridiculous rules,' Miss Quinn says under her breath.

'Paul's just – different,' I say, trying to explain.

'I know, Hannah,' she says. 'I've noticed, in class, the other kids like to wind him up. I won't have that, of course, but there won't always be a teacher around to sort things out. He is OK, isn't he? He's not unhappy?'

I frown. Paul *is* unhappy. You can see it in his eyes, in the way he walks, even the way he smiles. It's been there all along, right from the first moment we met. It's something the shell can't disguise, and it may even be the reason Murphy and the others give him such a hard time. He's like a little kid with *kick me* scrawled in chalk across the back of his coat.

'Paul's had a rough time, Miss,' I say. 'In the past, y'know. But he's OK now. He *is* settling in.'

'Well, tell him that if he has any problems, he can always come to me,' Miss Quinn says. 'Sometimes it helps to talk.'

'Sure.'

'Are the two of you busy after school?' she asks then. 'If you had a couple of afternoons to spare, you could work on the portrait after half three. I mean, Paul may not fancy that, especially after all the detentions, but . . .'

'I'll ask him, Miss,' I say. 'I think he'll be up for it.'

'Excellent,' says Miss Quinn, sipping her coffee. 'I'm usually around till at least five. Come any day you like – and bring your own Cherryade!'

So, most days, Paul and I fall into the habit of staying after school to work on the portrait. Some days, Miss Quinn pulls the blinds shut and sets up a spotlight to make a strong light–dark contrast, and I sit there for an hour at a time, my face warm from the spotlight, staring into space, dreaming.

In the background, Miss Quinn wanders about the room setting up still-life arrangements, mounting artwork, marking homework or filling in progress sheets. Sometimes, she comes over and looks at the portrait, nodding, smiling. Other times she points out a way Paul could improve things.

One Tuesday afternoon, I get to the art room to

find Miss Quinn on her way out, a bundle of files and papers under her arm.

'There's a staff meeting today, Hannah,' she tells me. 'I won't be back over till five or so, but you and Paul are welcome to use the room. OK?'

'Right, Miss, no problem.'

The door shuts behind her. I wait for Paul, but there's no sign of him. We agreed to come up today, but maybe he's forgotten? I slouch down the stairs and out into the deserted courtyard. I sit on a low wall for a while, soaking up the spring sun, but there's nobody around at all.

I wonder if maybe Paul has committed some extra-evil crime and been punished with a rare after-school detention? He had black nail varnish on this morning, I remember. I walk over to the main school building and sneak down beside the hall windows, standing on tiptoes to peer inside.

McKenzie stands on the stage, pointing at a flip chart and waving his arms around, while three rows of staff snooze quietly in front of him. Staff meeting. No detentions today – except for the teachers.

Paul must have headed home on the bus. I'm kind of hacked off with him, but there's not a lot I can do. I decide to head up to the high street to kill some time and wait for the five o'clock bus home. I cut across the grass, because there are no teachers about to tell me I can't, and head down towards the kitchen block on the way to the car-park exit.

I'm right beside the big kitchen bins before I realize there's something going on, and by then it's too late. I've found Paul and I've found Kit and I've found Murphy, Tom and Fergus. I wish to God I hadn't, but it's too late – they've seen me, and I've seen them, and my face flares scarlet and I feel sick. I'm shaking, and I can't tell whether it's from fear or anger.

'Hannah,' says Kit, coming towards me, taking my arm. 'You shouldn't be here.'

I pull away from his touch as though it burns me. I look at my brother, his smiling face, his dark hair spiked up carefully, just the way Joey likes it. If she could see him now, she'd never find anything to like about him again.

My brother puts his hands up, palm outwards, still smiling.

'It's OK, Hannah,' he says. 'Nothing to worry about. There's been a bit of bother, but I've got it all under control now. Just clear off and we'll talk about it later.'

But I know I don't want to talk to Kit about this, not now, not later, not ever.

Behind him, Murphy, Tom and Fergus are crouched round a figure lying curled up on the gravel, his blazer grey with dust, his green hair splotched with red. Blood?

I knew they kicked footballs at him, I knew they called him names, I knew they trashed his stuff and tripped him up and flicked bubblegum into his hair, but this is something else.

And whatever he says, Kit is not here as a spectator.

I try to shove past him, but he grabs my arm and hangs on tight, and I can't. '*PAUL!*' I shriek.

Murphy turns round, his face a mask of leering spite and anger. 'What's *she* doing here?' he rages. 'Man, she had better keep her mouth shut, or . . .'

'She will,' says Kit smoothly, before Murphy can finish the threat. 'She will.'

Murphy sneers at me and spits on to the gravel. 'We're finished here,' he says. 'C'mon, lads, let's go.'

He gets up, brushes down his trousers, grabs up his bag. The others follow suit, not meeting my eye. 'Coming, Kit?' Murphy asks, and Kit lets go of my arm roughly and follows them.

I stand still till they reach the gate. Murphy turns back, laughing. 'See you around, Muppet-boy!' he shouts as they walk away.

I run to Paul and kneel down beside him. His body is crumpled, folded up on itself, shaking slightly. His arms are wrapped tightly round his face. There's a stink of something overpoweringly sweet and sickly, like cheap perfume.

'Paul,' I whisper. 'It's me, Hannah. It's OK. They've all gone.'

He makes a low, whimpering sound that grips my heart.

I touch his hair, the red splotches that are dripping down on to the gravel. It's sticky, but it doesn't feel like blood. It's more like . . . *jam*?

I look around and I can see an empty jam jar under the kitchen bins. There are other things scattered across the gravel too. An empty perfume bottle, a blusher brush, a pot of something green and glittery.

'Paul,' I whisper again. 'Did they hurt you? Are you hurt?'

He shakes his head, still hiding behind his arms.

'Do you want me to fetch a teacher? Miss Quinn?'

'No!' Paul's voice chokes out. 'I want you to go away!'

'But I'm trying to help you!' I cry, stricken. 'I'm your friend! Paul, you have to tell me what they did.'

He jerks away from me, struggling into a sitting position, his face still hidden.

'I can't,' he says raggedly.

'Paul . . .'

I pull at his hands, one at a time, dragging them away from his face. Murphy and his mates have painted Paul's mouth with a wide, crimson gash of lipstick, smudged and smeared. His eyes are ringed with the green glitter stuff and his cheeks are painted with vivid pink circles of blusher, like a pantomime dame. His hair is dripping with jam, and someone has stuck a dark-red rose behind his ear.

I bite my lip, appalled.

I drag a handful of tissues out of my bag and try to dab at his face, but he snatches them away from me. 'Please, Hannah,' he gasps. 'Let me do this. I want to be on my own. Please?'

Then I see the tears that have mixed in with the glitter and the lipstick and the jam, and I back off slowly.

'Go home, Hannah,' he says gruffly. 'Go home.'

I go.

CHAPTER 20

'You must have got it wrong, Hannah,' says Joey. 'Kit would never be a part of something so mean. He's been trying to *stop* the bullies. He doesn't like Paul, but he'd never do something like *that*.'

She perches on the window sill, her skinny legs in long, stripy socks hooked over the back of my computer chair. I lie stretched out on my bed, head propped in my hands. It feels like the end of the world.

'I didn't get it wrong, Joey,' I tell her. 'You know I didn't.'

When I rang Beachcomber Cottage earlier, Paul was just back. 'He can't come to the phone,' Joey told me. 'He's in the shower. Apparently he was messing about on that mad bike and fell into some rubbish bins up in town. He stinks. And he's in a foul mood – nearly bit my head off.'

'No,' I explained. 'No, Joey, that's not what happened. It was nothing to do with the bike.'

'But Paul . . .'

'Come over, Joey,' I said.

We sit in my room, waiting for Kit to come home.

'I don't get it,' Joey says, frowning. 'Where *is* he? It's past nine o'clock. He said he had footy training after school, and then he wanted a night in to revise, because there's some kind of S2 French test tomorrow.'

'There *was* no footy training after school,' I point out. 'I bet there's no French test, either.'

'But why would Kit lie to me?' Joey moans.

'You know why.'

'I can't believe it,' she says, but she does believe it. I can see it in her eyes, dark blue and shining with unshed tears. I can see it in her pale face, the way she sits on the window sill, edgy, brittle, anxious.

'Do you think he's been lying to us all along?' I ask. 'Kit? Do you think he only pretended to get Murphy and the others to back off? Maybe he's been hassling Paul the whole time.'

'No way,' says Joey listlessly. 'No way. Paul is my *foster-brother.*'

'Look, Kit is way out of order on this,' I point

out. 'I don't know if he's been involved all along, but trust me, he's involved now. Murphy and the others have had a downer on Paul right from the start. What they did to him, Joey – it was awful. Just because he's . . . well, different.'

'What's wrong with being different?'

'Nothing,' I shrug. 'But there's something about Paul that Kit and his mates just can't handle.'

'What?' Joey demands. 'I just don't get it.'

I don't want to get it, either, but I saw what Kit and Murphy did to Paul and I got the message, loud and clear.

'They're trying to make out that he's gay,' I say at last, putting into words the fear that's been eating away at me for weeks. 'He makes them nervous – they think he's a threat.'

'Idiots!' Joey snorts. 'Boys! They are so insecure, so paranoid. Paul isn't gay. As if!'

I blink. 'You . . . you don't think he could be, then?' I ask. 'I mean, you can tell me if he is. It won't make any difference. I'll always be his mate.'

'Hannah, sometimes I despair of you,' Joey says. 'Don't you notice what's going on around you? Can't you see? Paul isn't gay, whatever that bunch of neds thinks. I know he isn't, OK?'

'How do you know?'

'Because he's mad about you,' Joey says. 'That's why.'

My heart thuds and my cheeks flame scarlet. Joey is wrong – she has to be. Paul is my friend, I know that, but not once has he given me the slightest sign that he's looking for anything more than that.

'No way,' I whisper.

'Way,' Joey replies. 'Trust me. Way.'

The door slams downstairs, and we hear Kit talking to Mum and Dad. An aroma of toasted cheese wafts gently up the stairs.

Joey sighs. 'I've been a useless friend lately.'

'No . . .'

'Yes,' she corrects me. 'Don't argue, Hannah. Nobody argues with Joey Donovan.'

We hear footsteps on the stairs, and Joey creeps out on to the landing, holding a finger to her lips. I sit on the bed, hugging my knees.

'Hey,' says Kit, a little warily. 'Joey! I didn't think you were coming over tonight, or I'd have been home sooner.'

'To revise?' Joey asks sweetly.

'Revise? Oh, yeah,' Kit bluffs. 'It's just that the footy went on a bit, and a few of us went back to Tom's to discuss tactics for next week's game. We kind of forgot the time.'

'Drop the act, Kit, I know what happened,' Joey says coldly. 'I saw Paul.'

'What a *grass* that loser is,' Kit says in disgust. 'Might have known he'd go bleating to you.'

'He didn't.'

'Hannah, then,' says Kit. 'Look, you weren't there, Joey, you didn't see. He winds us up the whole time. He was asking for it.'

'And you just happened to have lippy, perfume, blusher, eyeshadow and jam handy to teach him a lesson. Is that it?'

There's a long silence, and I'm tempted to peek out on to the landing just in case Kit is weeping silent tears of shame, or trying to distract Joey with a quick snog. When I open the door a crack, though, he's just eating cheese on toast and staring her out like he couldn't care less.

'You are *so* not the boy I thought you were,' Joey says at last.

Kit shrugs.

'Just stay away from me and my family, Kit Murray.'

'My pleasure,' he says. 'Bunch of weirdos.'

His door slams shut, and a blast of loud, jangly music erupts suddenly. Joey is still on the landing, trembling slightly. She looks round and catches my eye.

'I hate my brother,' I whisper to her.

She smiles sadly and grabs up her coat from the banisters.

'Me too,' she says.

CHAPTER 21

The next day, Joey sits beside me on the school bus and Kit sits at the back, the way he used to. He's in a mean mood today, scowling and snapping at everyone and shooting me poisonous looks like I'm the one who did something wrong.

Paul isn't on the bus at all. Joey says he told Jed and Eva he felt ill, and stayed in bed. 'I tried to talk to him last night, but he wouldn't open the door,' she tells me. 'He told me to go away.'

'He said that to me, when I found him.'

'He must be feeling awful,' Joey says. 'Those losers have really dented his confidence. He'll get over it, though. Give him a couple of days.'

I hope she's right.

Joey has parcelled up the valentine CD Kit burned

for her, the skull-and-crossbones silver ring and the swirly bracelet he bought her instead of chocolate for Easter. She gives the parcel to me, to leave in Kit's room. She is wiping him out of her life.

Pity I don't have that option.

Later, in art, Miss Quinn asks if Paul and I are coming in after school to finish the painting. 'Monday is the last day for sending stuff in,' she explains. 'I've made a window-mount for it, and filled in the entry form. If he could just finish it off . . .'

'Paul is ill,' I say. 'He's not in school.'

'Oh, dear,' says Miss Quinn. Her shoulders droop with disappointment.

We look over at the painting, taped with brown gum strip to an A2 drawing board at the side of the classroom. It's not like looking at me any more. The portrait has taken on an identity of its own. A brown-haired girl with startled, brown eyes looks back at you as though she's seeing something nobody else can see. Only the neck and body remain unpainted, giving the picture an uneasy, lopsided look.

'It's good,' Joey says, squinting at the picture. 'Do you think it could get a prize?'

'Perhaps,' Miss Quinn says. 'I'd certainly have liked to put it forward. Never mind.'

'Paul would want it to be entered,' Joey states

firmly. 'He's ill, but it's probably just one of those twenty-four-hour bug things. I'll take the painting home, Miss. He can finish it there.'

'Oh, d'you think so?' Miss Quinn's face lights up. 'It might be worth a try! Paul's folder is somewhere here . . .'

'It'll cheer him up,' Joey whispers to me. 'He loves painting, and you heard Miss Quinn – this might win a prize. That'd show those boneheads, wouldn't it?'

After school, we trudge back to Beachcomber Cottage, Joey carrying Paul's art folder and me carrying a bag of acrylic paints and some brand-new brushes from the stock cupboard. I feel shy about seeing Paul after what Joey said, but right now he needs a friend, and I'm not about to let him down.

Paul is alone, huddled at the kitchen table sipping a mug of miso soup. Miso soup is Eva's remedy for all ills. It looks like warm, grey dishwater with strands of edible seaweed floating about in it, and tastes pretty much the same. I'm not sure if it can cure bullying.

'We brought your portrait home,' Joey announces. 'Miss Quinn says it has to be finished by Monday.'

Paul groans. 'Joey, I'm not in the mood,' he mumbles.

'C'mon, you're not ill, are you?' she asks brutally.

'You can't just mope around feeling sorry for yourself. You can't just let them *win*.'

I sit down next to Paul and fall into the portrait pose, one hand at my collar, one hand in my lap. I pull a frantic, staring face, tongue lolling. Paul rolls his eyes and hides behind his soup, but his lips twitch with the hint of a smile. Krusty leaps up on to my shoulder and swishes her tail for a moment before stretching out round my neck.

'Hey, Krusty,' I tell her, dropping the gurny face. 'You're not in this picture. Stop trying to hog the limelight.'

Joey hands Paul the folder and I push the bag of acrylic paints towards him.

'Give me a break,' he says.

'No!' snaps Joey. 'You don't need a break. You need to get up, fix a smile on your face and get back to school, show those gimps you can't be beaten. Hold your head up, Paul. Be yourself.'

'I have been, Joey,' he sighs. 'That's the bit they have a problem with.'

'Yeah, but it's *their* problem,' I point out. 'You can't let them think it's OK to treat you like this. It isn't. You have to tell Jed and Eva, or Miss Quinn or even McKenzie. You can't let them just get *away* with it.'

'I'm not a grass,' he says. 'Back off. I'll deal with it.'

'Sure,' I say.

'Wise up,' Joey rages. 'Get mad. Fight back. Get your *act* together, Paul!'

Paul takes a deep breath and picks up the folder. He takes out the painting, chewing his lip, then checks through the bag of paints and brushes. 'I'm doing it for Miss Quinn,' he says sulkily. 'Not you.'

'I don't care if you do it for world peace, just do it,' Joey huffs.

'I've said I will, haven't I?'

'School on Monday?' she asks.

Paul walks over to the sink to get a jar of water and an old saucer to mix the paint. 'Don't push your luck,' he says.

Joey grins, switches on her CD player at full volume and breaks open the biscuit tin.

'Wow,' says Miss Quinn, taking the portrait out of its folder on Monday morning. 'Paul, this is . . . wonderful. Thank you.'

Paul is sitting on the table, watching Miss Quinn. He still looks kind of fragile, but he's smiling, his cheeks faintly pink with pleasure. He's pleased with the picture, I know. He decided to paint in Krusty as she slept, curled round my shoulders, and he's captured the softness of her silky fur perfectly. The whole painting looks sort of surreal now, unexpected, compelling.

'The cat is brilliant,' Miss Quinn says. 'Exactly what it needed. Is it one of the kittens, Hannah?'

I nod. 'She snuggles up round my neck the whole time,' I explain.

'She's a star,' says Miss Quinn. She fetches a scalpel from the desk drawer and cuts the painting off its drawing board, then turns it over and tapes it into a pre-cut window-mount, fixing the form with Paul's name, age and school on to the back.

The painting is cool. A girl who looks a little like me stares out of the picture with wide, faraway eyes, one hand touching a tortoiseshell kitten curled round her neck. She looks beautiful and sad and dreamy, while behind her the wide grey ocean crashes and churns.

'Not invisible,' says Paul as we leave the classroom to head for registration.

'No,' I agree. 'Not any more.'

CHAPTER 22

I sit on the beach with Paul, watching the tide lap in. The water slides forward like skeins of white silk, then falls back, swirling. It seeps into a sand message, rushes past a tiny cairn of stones, shells and feathers. The feathers are lifted on the tide, carried away.

Krusty, her whiskers quivering with excitement, is stalking a seagull four times her size. Her bottom wiggles a bit as she creeps forward, and her fur ruffles in the breeze.

'I can't do this any more,' Paul says.

'What? The beach magic?'

'Not any of it,' Paul replies. 'I'm too tired. I've had enough.'

I look at him, hunched up against the sea wall

with his head thrown back, eyes closed, lashes dark against pale skin.

I don't know what to do. Even when things are bad, Paul always manages to shrug off his worries, convince me it'll be OK. He can cheer me up with a swig of Cherryade or a scribbled drawing or a ride on the zebra-striped bike, fix anything with a message in the sand or a stone skimmed out across the water.

Since the incident by the kitchen bins, though, the fight has gone out of him. He looks fragile, and there are dark shadows under his eyes that I've never seen before.

He has stopped travelling on the school bus. Instead, he rides to the pool every morning on the zebra-striped bike, swims for an hour and carries right on to school. He arrives early, too early for Murphy to be lying in wait. After school, he hangs out in the art room, waiting till everyone has gone before cycling home.

'It's school, isn't it?' I ask.

'What do you think?'

'They haven't done anything – anything *bad* – again, though?'

Paul shakes his head. 'It's just – it's just knowing that they hate me,' he says softly. 'I can't stand it. I really thought I could settle here. I thought I could have friends – you, Joey, maybe even Kit. It's all gone pear-shaped, as usual. Nothing ever lasts.'

His hand closes round mine, clumsily, his palm dry and cool. I try not to faint with shock. Do friends hold hands?

'I get stuff wrong,' Paul is saying. 'All the time. I try so hard, but I still mess up.'

'Doesn't matter,' I say, giving his hand a squeeze. 'Not to me.'

'I know, Hannah, not to you. You believe in me. You always have. I wish – well, I wish things had been different.'

'Me too,' I whisper. 'We can still fix it, Paul. We can still make it OK.'

'Nah.' He sighs. 'Not now.'

Krusty skitters up beside us, dragging a huge strip of seaweed, the kind that looks like a giant's dreadlocks. She settles down in Paul's lap, and he lets go of my hand to stroke her. I feel like my heart is breaking.

'Joey told me to get my act together,' he says. 'I'm trying, Hannah, but I'm scared. I'm sick of acting like I don't care when they tell me I'm dirt. I'm sick of acting like it doesn't hurt when they laugh at me, sneer at me, shove me, kick me. It hurts, OK?'

Paul is staring out at the ocean, his eyes filmed with tears. I have never seen a boy cry before, at least, not since junior school. It feels awful.

'Don't let them win, Paul,' I tell him. 'They don't hate you, they just don't . . . understand. Losers.'

'How about Kit?' he asks.

What can I say? Kit is the biggest loser of all.

It's art, and Joey and I are dyeing batiks in a big bucket of turquoise dye that sits in one of the sinks. Joey pushes the fabric into the dye with rubber-gloved hands while I stir everything round with a big wooden spoon. It's last period on a Friday, and I'm hoping to fish my batik out of the dye bucket before the bell goes.

'Hey,' says Joey, nodding down towards the courtyard below us. 'What's Paul doing out of class?'

He's walking fast, hunched over, hands in pockets, raggedy hair swinging.

'Dunno.' I frown. 'On an errand?'

But Paul cuts across the courtyard and unchains the zebra-striped bike. 'What's he *doing*?' asks Joey.

I drop my wooden spoon into the dye bath. 'Miss Quinn? Could I go to the loo, please?'

'Sure,' Miss Quinn says. 'Don't be long.'

I take the stairs two steps at a time, sprinting out into the courtyard just as Paul pedals by. I run in front of the zebra-striped bike and he stops short, refusing to look me in the eye.

'You should be in class,' I tell him.

'And?' says Paul.

'So why aren't you? Did something happen?'

'I walked out,' he says softly. 'Kit and Murphy were hassling me again. Messing with my school bag, kicking my chair, flicking bits of pastry dough left over from HE. No big deal. But they've taken my sketchbook.'

He picks absently at a patch of grey pastry dough stuck to his black combats.

'So?' I push him. 'We can get it back.'

'Hannah, you don't understand,' Paul says. 'I've had enough. Game over.'

'What d'you mean, game over?' I ask, alarmed.

Paul shrugs. 'It's over. It happened, I couldn't deal with it and now it's over. It's over because I give up, OK?'

'Paul, I want you to tell Miss Quinn what's going on,' I say. 'Come up with me now. She'll find somewhere quiet to talk to you. She'll listen; she'll believe you. You can't keep this quiet any more, you just can't.'

'OK,' Paul says. 'Suppose I tell. Do you know what'll happen? Miss Quinn will tell Jed and Eva, and they'll tell my social workers – they'd have to. They'll talk to the school and talk to the Donovans and decide that this placement isn't working out, and I'll be back in Glasgow before you know it, stuck in some new care home.'

'You don't know that,' I argue.

'Hannah, I do. It's happened before,' he says sadly. 'Just let me deal with this my own way. I'm gonna ride around a bit, think things through.'

'Want a passenger?' I ask lightly.

'No, Hannah. Not today.'

He turns the zebra-striped bike and pedals away, past the science block and right out through the main gates.

There's a sick feeling in the pit of my stomach, a churning, dragging ache that says there's something very wrong. Sunshine beats down across the courtyard, but I'm as cold as ice.

CHAPTER 23

My mobile rings at half eight, just as dusk falls headlong into darkness. It's Joey, asking if I've seen Paul.

'I told Eva he'd just be at yours,' she says, 'watching TV or drawing or drinking Cherryade, whatever. You know how she worries.'

'He's not here, Joey,' I tell her.

'Oh. Well, he's probably still riding around on that loopy bike, then, thinking,' Joey decides. 'He wanted to be on his own, didn't he?'

'It's dark,' I say, stating the obvious.

'I know, but it's not *late* or anything,' Joey reasons. 'He'll be OK, won't he? Is Kit at home?'

'No, he's out with the lads.'

'You don't suppose . . .'

'Joey, don't stress,' I scold her. 'You're getting as bad as Eva. Paul wanted some time alone, to think. He'll be back soon.'

I press the button to end the call, but that sick feeling is back. I tell myself to be calm, to keep working, get the school stuff out of the way like I always do on Fridays, so I can relax and enjoy the weekend. I can't. I flop down on to the bed, flip open my phone again and punch out Kit's mobile number.

There's a whole lot of crashing and rumbling in the background, so I guess he's at the skatepark.

'Kit,' I say.

'Hannah. What do *you* want?' he asks rudely.

'Is Paul with you?'

'Why would that loser be with *me*?' Kit demands. 'He's not exactly my best mate, in case you hadn't noticed.'

'Oh, I'd noticed all right,' I tell him. 'He hasn't been home. I wondered if you and your little gang of heavies had seen him, that's all.'

'Not since he stormed out of geography class this afternoon,' Kit laughs. 'He has no sense of humour. Wimp, or what?'

'Well, thank you for your kind words, Kit,' I say. 'I feel so much better for talking to you.'

'Get lost, Hannah,' he snaps, and the phone goes dead.

I walk over to the window, lift the curtain and press my face against the glass. Paul is out there, somewhere. He's cycling around in the dark on a bike with no lights, thinking about how come he's messed up again. A new school, a new start, new friends – but some things never change. Paul carries his bad luck around with him, like an invisible cloud.

My breath has steamed up the glass, and I trace his name in the condensation. 'Come back,' I whisper. 'Please.'

But no matter how hard I stare into the darkness, there's nobody there. I switch the light out and lie on my bed in the dark, waiting for the squeak of a home-made bike on the pathway outside. Instead, I hear the phone ringing downstairs, and Dad's voice in the hallway talking to the caller. 'Hannah?' he shouts up to me. 'Can you come down a minute?'

I drift out to the top of the stairs.

'Have you seen Paul?' Dad asks me. 'It's Eva. He hasn't been home for tea and they're getting worried. Did he say anything to you about where he might be?'

I come down the stairs, sink down on the bottom step just across from Dad. He hands me the phone.

Eva's voice is frantic. 'It's not like him,' she tells me. 'He always tells us where he's going. He's never been this late. Have you seen him, Hannah? Has he said anything to you?'

Game over, he said to me. *I give up*.

'No, no, not really,' I say.

'Was he OK earlier?' Eva presses. 'At school?'

'Er . . . I think so,' I bluff.

Dad is giving me a frowny, serious look that makes his forehead all lined and wrinkly. 'If you know anything, tell her,' he whispers. 'They're going to call the police if he's not in by ten.'

The police?

'He wanted to be alone,' I say to Eva. 'He had a rough day at school. He said he was just going to ride his bike around and think. I asked if he wanted company, but he didn't. I'm sorry, Eva, that's all I know.'

'What do you mean, a rough day?' Eva questions. 'Paul is happy at school. He's settled in well. Hasn't he?'

I can't answer her. I hold out the phone to Dad.

'Good luck, Eva,' I hear him say. 'Call us if you hear anything, or if there's anything we can do. Anything at all.'

I sit by the phone, willing it to ring again, but there's no more news. Kit comes in at half ten, and Dad sits him down and quizzes him about Paul.

'Why would I know anything?' he says, scowling.

'No reason,' I shoot back, and he flushes red.

'It's not as if I even liked the guy,' he snaps. 'He's a total weirdo.'

'Kit!' Dad roars. 'The lad has had a very tough time. He's lost his mum, been taken into care, passed around from pillar to post. Is it any wonder he's a bit troubled? Show some respect!'

'Sorr-ee!'

'Eva is worried sick,' Mum chips in. 'They're getting the police in, and I don't blame them. The Donovans can't think of any reason why he'd just disappear like that. Can you?'

'No, I *told* you,' says Kit. 'I haven't seen him since school. He walked out of geography and Mr Worrall reported him to McKenzie. He's in big trouble. He's probably scared to face Jed and Eva, thinks he can run away or something. He'll turn up.'

'Let's hope so,' Mum sighs. 'You two had best get to bed. I expect it'll all be sorted out by morning.'

We go upstairs. On the landing, I turn to face Kit. 'You'd better tell me if you know anything,' I hiss. 'If you or your bonehead mates have been hassling him again, if you've *touched* him . . .'

'We haven't!' protests Kit. 'Like I said, the last I saw him was in geography. We were only having a laugh – we didn't mean any harm. It's not my fault he can't take a joke!'

'Nothing's ever your fault, is it?' I snap.

Kit looks angry, but scared too. 'Hannah, you have to keep quiet about all this stuff at school,' he says. 'It's nothing serious. There's no point raking it up, getting us into trouble, not with the police poking around. OK? Keep your mouth shut.'

'Why should I?'

My brother reaches out a hand in the dark, touches my arm. His fingers are trembling.

'Please?' he says.

CHAPTER 24

It's like being in the middle of a nightmare. We sit round the table at Beachcomber Cottage, sipping tea that's too stewed and too sweet, listening for the phone. The phone stays silent.

Paul has been missing since yesterday afternoon, and now it is nine fifteen on Saturday morning. They found the zebra-striped bike on the coast road down by the headland, abandoned by the side of the road. So where is Paul?

A policewoman, who looks too young and too chirpy to be dealing with this case, tells us she is confident they'll have a lead before too long, but can any of us kids remember anything that could explain why Paul might want to disappear? Anything at all?

'Son?' Dad prompts. 'You said something about

Paul walking out of class yesterday. Perhaps he's worried he might be in trouble for that?'

'He walked out of geography,' Kit says dully. 'He just got up, grabbed his rucksack and walked out of the door. Mr Worrall went after him and asked him what he was playing at, and Paul just said he'd had enough.'

'Enough of what?' the policewoman wonders, scribbling rapidly.

'Haven't a clue,' says Kit.

Mikey drifts off from the table, teasing Itchy and Scratchy with a wisp of tinsel tied to a string. They leap and swipe at it, and Mikey lies down on the floor with them, rolling, laughing. It could be any other day at Beachcomber Cottage, but it's not. It's today, the worst day of my life.

'Paul's happy here,' Eva is saying. 'He likes school. He has friends. We know there've been problems in the past, but he *is* settled here, isn't he, Joey?'

Joey looks at me uneasily. We made a promise, but it's one that's getting harder and harder to keep.

'I think so,' she mutters.

'Not really,' I say at the same time, and everyone turns to look at me. Jed and Eva are wide-eyed and anxious, Dad is frowning, Kit is fizzing, but Joey shrugs and nods as if to tell me I'm doing the right thing.

Krusty shifts around in my lap, blinking at me

with dark eyes that give nothing away. I run my hand over her fur, feel the rattle of her purr.

'Hannah?' Dad says, touching my sleeve. 'Tell us what you mean.'

So I tell them about Paul. I tell them about how the lads started to tease him, and how the teasing got worse and worse until it was just about every minute of every day.

'Just little things,' I explain. 'A football kicked at him hard, on purpose. Bubblegum flicked into his hair. A push when he was on the stairs. And worse things too. Paul had no friends, apart from me and Joey. He hated school.'

Kit squirms around in his chair, unable to meet my eye.

'Why didn't he tell us?' Eva cries. 'Why didn't he say? We could have stopped it! We could have sorted it!'

'He made us promise,' says Joey. 'He said that if the social workers got to hear, he'd be taken away again, and he didn't want that. He wanted to stay, Eva, that's why he kept quiet.'

'Oh, God!' Eva says. Jed puts an arm round her.

There's a long silence, and then there's a shrill ringtone and the policewoman snaps open her mobile. We watch her nodding, listening, making one-word answers. We watch the smile slide off her face.

My heart is thumping as she shuts the mobile and walks over to Jed and Eva.

'This may be nothing,' she says, 'but we'd like you to come down to the beach at the far end of the bay. We may have found Paul's bag, and a black sweater and a pair of black baseball boots . . .'

Eva makes a low, moaning sound like an animal in pain.

'We don't know anything yet, not for sure,' the policewoman says. 'He could be anywhere.'

'But you found his shoes,' Jed says raggedly.

'Let's get you down there, make sure they *are* Paul's shoes, before we start jumping to conclusions,' the policewoman says.

Everyone is jumping to conclusions anyway. Eva is sobbing, and Jed has buried his face in his hands. They think Paul has drowned.

'What's wrong with you all?' I burst out. 'Stop thinking he's dead! Paul wouldn't. He wouldn't. He *never* swims in the sea. He says it's too dangerous!'

Jed stands up, rubbing at his forehead as if to make the bad thoughts disappear. 'Paul's fascinated by the sea, but he's afraid of it too,' he whispers. 'Because of what happened to his mother.'

'She went away,' I whisper. 'She left him.'

'No, Hannah,' says Jed. 'Is that what he told you? That's not what happened. Paul's mum was ill with depression. She didn't go away – she drowned. She left her clothes and shoes in a pile on the beach and walked into the sea.'

'She killed herself,' Kit breathes. 'No way.'

All the bones in my body turn to water. I sit down heavily on a driftwood chair, my stomach soured with a sick, hollow ache. My head is a tangle of pictures I don't want to see. A cat called Splodge, a message in a bottle, a little boy who sat at home for hours, maybe days, waiting for his mum to come home.

'Let's go and take a look at those clothes,' the policewoman says into the silence. She ushers Jed and Eva outside. Dad, the only adult left, jumps up and starts to clear the table, rinsing mugs under the tap.

'No news is good news,' he says brightly. But he's not kidding anyone. Itchy and Scratchy slink silently on to the tabletop, mopping up biscuit crumbs, and nobody cares enough to chase them away.

'Play football?' Mikey asks, tugging Kit's hoodie, but Kit is slumped at the table, his face white.

'I'll give you a game, mate,' Dad says, and he bundles Mikey out into the garden, leaving Joey, Kit and me alone in the kitchen. Nobody can find a single word to say.

'I didn't know,' Kit chokes out eventually. 'I didn't realize.'

Joey turns on him, her eyes blazing. 'Didn't care, more like,' she rages. 'You couldn't leave him alone, could you? You and your stupid mates.'

Kit reaches into his jacket and brings out a small, black book. 'It was only meant to be a joke,' he says. 'Murphy was showing it round the class, having a laugh. I thought he'd give it back, but he didn't, he chucked it in the bins on the way out of school. I got it back for him. Tell Paul that, yeah?'

'If I ever see him again,' Joey snaps.

I pick up the little black book, flick through pages that are stained, now, with drips of cola and leaky biro.

Inside the back cover are pages of drawings of me, Joey and Kit, vivid, scribbled sketches like the ones we saw of Kit in Paul's other sketchbook, the day of the snow war. The day it all went wrong. They weren't stalky, weirdo sketches, the way Kit thought. They were roughs for the three cat characters in Paul's story.

At the front of the book is the story I glimpsed that day on the beach – a comic-strip story about a sad-eyed boy and three cat-heroes. KoolKat, that's Kit. KrazyKat, that's Joey. And KittenKat, me.

The sad-eyed boy – well, that's Paul, of course.

He came from the land beyond the sea, Paul has written. *His feet and fingers were webbed, his skin was silver with scales, his hair was made of soft, green seaweed . . .*

I flick further and find cruel, dog-faced characters who look like Murphy, Tom and Fergus. Later in the book, KoolKat turns traitor and joins them. The book isn't finished. The last drawing shows the dog-faced kids chasing Paul towards the sea, but it's just a rough sketch, mapped out with light pencil lines. You can't tell what's going to happen.

I look again at the pictures of me. I've seen that little cat face before, on a torn bit of tracing paper, a home-made tattoo. And on a black envelope too, covered in stars and spirals in Joey's silver pen – but it wasn't from Joey, of course. It was from Paul. The valentine was for me. He even bought another KitKat for me, because Kit snaffled the first one.

'I can't stand this,' Joey bursts out, staring out of the window. 'What's he playing at, leaving his clothes on the beach? What are we meant to think?'

'He's a strong swimmer,' Kit says.

'Not that strong. Besides, where would he swim *to*?'

There is nowhere to swim to. Once you're past Seal Island, there's nothing but miles and miles of empty ocean, shining and sparkling under an open sky as the earth tilts westwards.

Seal Island. Paul once called it the land beyond the sea. He told me that seals were the spirits of those who had drowned in the ocean . . .

'Seal Island!' I say. 'He's gone to Seal Island!'

'What?' Joey asks. 'How do you . . . ?'

'I just know, OK? We have to tell the police. We have to find him. Quick!'

Krusty leaps down as I jump up from the table. We don't stop to tell Dad and Mikey; we don't stop to think. We run outside and out across the field to the beach. There's a little knot of police officers huddled with Jed and Eva at the far end, beneath the little headland, and we stumble over the dunes and down on to the wet sand, running towards them.

'These are his boots,' Eva is saying as we skid to a halt beside them. 'This is his stuff. Definitely.'

Paul's wrecked old baseball boots are lying on a rock just above the tideline, his black sweater and school bag piled up alongside. In the damp sand nearby, there's a circle of gull feathers with one perfect, tiny piece of driftwood in the centre. It's fragile and angular, spattered with patches of brown like a miniature snake.

One of the policemen is photographing everything; another takes clear plastic bags from a briefcase and starts collecting everything up. Evidence.

'I've thought of something,' I blurt out, through ragged breaths. 'I know where Paul went. He's at Seal Island. He used to call it *the land beyond the sea*, and he'd talk about how magical it was, with beaches all around . . .'

'No,' says Jed. 'Seal Island is too far for anyone to swim. There are currents too. If he tried . . .'

'Don't,' says Eva, biting her knuckles. She looks out at the grey shadow of island, and her eyes fill with hope.

'He's there,' I tell them again. 'I know he is. We have to go and look.'

One of the policemen pats my sleeve. 'We will, pet,' he says. 'We'll be checking out all the possibilities. We'll keep looking.'

'Now, though,' Joey cuts in. 'We need to look *now*.'

'All in good time,' the policeman says. 'Our search teams are already combing the beaches, and we've called out the coastguards too. They'll be here soon.'

'Best thing you can do is wait at the cottage,' Jed says. 'Stay by the phone, in case there's any news.'

We turn away.

'He's there,' I mutter. 'I know he is.'

'So we'll find him,' says Kit.

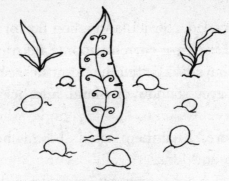

CHAPTER 25

Kit breaks into a run and we follow, scrambling up across the dunes to the field behind Beachcomber Cottage, the field where Jed's skanky old rowing boat lies upside down against the drystone wall. Krusty is crouched on the wall above it, her back arched, her tail swishing.

'We'll find him,' Kit says again. 'OK?'

I want to believe him, I really do.

He rolls the boat over, grabs up the oars and chucks them inside. As the dinghy rocks gently on the scrubby grass, Krusty lets out a long mewling noise and jumps in too.

'Not this time, little cat,' I tell her, but when I try to lift her out she slides through my fingers and jumps out of reach.

We grab on to the boat, hauling it down across the field, across the dunes, past the tideline, down over the damp sand and out into the water. The dinghy floats, swaying dangerously as Joey and I get in. Kit hangs on to the stern and pushes it out into the waves, dragging himself aboard once we're out of the shallows. He clambers on to the middle seat next to me and grabs one of the oars, while Joey sits hunched up in the bows, peering out towards the island.

'Get that cat out!' Kit huffs, but Krusty clings tight to my lap, burrowing in beneath my jumper. The boat turns slowly as we push the shoreline further and further away with each stroke of the oars.

'You kids!' a policeman roars from the beach. 'Get back here right now! One lost teenager is bad enough! Get back!'

We close our ears and row on. If we look back to the shore we can see the police search teams, in fluorescent yellow jackets, moving slowly along the sand to the left and the right of our beach. They have snifter dogs: big gruff German shepherds. They have already found Paul's bag and boots and sweater. What else can they be looking for? I block the question out of my head and pull on the oar.

It takes a long time to row to Seal Island, and as we row the hope ebbs away from me. Jed is right.

It's too far for anyone to swim, even a strong swimmer like Paul. Currents pull us off course several times. How much worse would it be for a swimmer, tired and cold and numb, inside and out?

'What's that?' Joey calls out as we draw close to the island. A big dark shape is slumped on the rocks to one side of the beach. It's big enough to be human, still enough to squeeze my heart with fear.

The boat nudges ashore beyond the rocks, and we drag it up across the sand before sprinting over to the rocks. There's a heavy splash and the dark shape is gone.

Only a seal.

There is no sign of life, except for a few curious seagulls wheeling overhead. No sign of Paul.

'Which way?' Joey asks. It's a tiny island, more of a rocky outcrop than anything else. If Paul is here, we'll find him. Krusty trots ahead, bottom wiggling, and Joey and I follow. Kit takes the opposite direction. We walk for five minutes and find nothing, and then I see it – a single white feather with a circle of white stones round it. My heart thuds.

'He's here,' I say. 'He is!'

A few steps further on there's a pyramid of driftwood sticks with a seaweed flag fluttering from the top, then a spiral of those tiny pink fingernail shells, pressed into the damp sand. My brother is up ahead, crouched on a rock, talking softly, like you would to a little kid you're trying not to scare.

I follow his gaze and see Paul, hunched up and shivering, his face grey, his thin shirt and trousers stained dark with the sea and white with the salt, his bare feet blue-white and crusted in sand. Even his green hair looks bleached out, more grey than emerald. There's a steep rock face behind him, and he leans back against it, curling into himself, hiding. His eyes are blank and empty, like there's nothing behind them.

'Paul, c'mon,' Kit is saying. 'It's time to go now. C'mon with me.'

Paul doesn't seem to hear.

'Just get him,' Joey says, exasperated, but Kit grabs on to her sleeve and pulls her back. She hasn't seen the flick knife in Paul's hand, the same knife I used to cut bubblegum from his hair a couple of weeks back. I know how sharp that knife is. I wish I didn't.

We're frozen to the spot, terrified to move in case it scares Paul into doing something stupid. I bend down and scoop Krusty up, gently but firmly.

Somewhere behind us there's the roar of a motor boat, and looking back towards the mainland I can see the big, grey coastguards' launch scudding across the waves towards us. Too late.

'Paul,' says Kit gently, 'put the knife down.'

Paul strokes the blade across his palm, his wrist, teasing. Suddenly I know why Paul always wears long sleeves, why he keeps his sweatbands on even in the swimming pool. I know what the knife is for, and my heart flips over.

'Put the knife down, mate,' Kit whispers.

'You're not my mate,' Paul snaps, and his eyes flash with hurt briefly before the emotion drains away again.

'Paul, I'm sorry,' Kit is saying. 'I let you down. I got scared. I got nervous. I didn't know how to handle things. I messed up big style.'

Kit tries to edge forward, but Paul huddles further into the rock face. 'Stay away,' he says, bringing the knife blade up to his lips.

Then Krusty squirms out of my grasp and bounds across the sand to Paul. She doesn't play safe, she doesn't hang back, she just runs up to Paul and claws her way up his legs, her tail swishing, and Paul drops the knife and reaches out to stroke her fur, lifting her up to his face, his shoulder.

'Hey, hey, little cat,' he says. 'What are you doing here?'

It's only when my breath comes out in a whoosh that I realize I've been holding it at all. Kit, Joey and I run forward, and Paul turns to face us like he only just realized we were there.

'Kind of early in the year for a sea swim,' Kit says, smiling.

Paul blinks, frowning, and then his green eyes hold Kit's gaze. 'Nah, it was no hassle,' he shrugs. 'What are you, some kind of wuss or what? Piece of cake.'

I bend down to pocket the flick knife, and Paul struggles to his feet. He's exhausted, shivering and unsteady on his feet, so Joey and I fling an arm each round him and together the whole bunch of us walk down to the water's edge, just as the coastguard launch runs ashore.

CHAPTER 26

It happened just the way Paul said it would. The social workers, when they turned up, said that the foster placement with Jed and Eva was clearly not working. Paul was a very disturbed boy, they said, more mixed-up than anyone had realized. He'd be better off back in Glasgow, at the children's home, where he could be reassessed, offered one-to-one counselling and helped to come to terms with his past. They planned to teach him in some kind of special unit for kids who couldn't cope with proper school.

Jed and Eva appealed against the decision, of course, but the odds were stacked against Paul. The social workers talked to Kit and got a full statement about the bullying, from start to finish. Kit was honest about it, even though it showed him up in a pretty poor light. The social workers talked to the teachers at Kirklaggan High too. They mostly said that Paul hadn't really fitted in, hadn't tried to, with the exception of Miss Quinn who said Paul was the most talented student she'd had the privilege to teach for a very long time.

They kept asking Paul why he hadn't asked for help, but he just kept saying that he didn't want to wreck things, didn't want to go back to the children's home. That was why he'd stayed quiet, but guess what? They took him back anyway.

That was a while ago now.

I didn't cope so well after Paul went away, not at first. I felt so guilty, so bad. I couldn't help thinking I could have done something different, something that could have stopped it all from going wrong. I hung around at the beach and collected feathers and shells and bits of seaglass to weave beach-magic spells, but nothing worked. Nothing seemed to cut through the fog of regret those first few weeks.

Then one afternoon I got home from school and found a skinny tortoiseshell cat curled up in the washing basket, and from then on the fog began to lift. Mum had finally caved in and talked to Eva, and that was that – Krusty moved in.

She always *was* my cat, right from the start.

I'd like to say she is perfectly behaved and that my mum has grown to love her, but that wouldn't be true. Krusty climbs the curtains and sharpens her claws on the furniture, and sometimes we come down in the morning and find feathers or tails or other scary things on the kitchen floor.

'Not another takeaway,' Dad says, and Mum huffs and gets out the disinfectant spray.

Krusty doesn't care. She snuggles in round my neck like a soft fur scarf, or curls up in Mum's shopping bag or on top of the TV, where it's nice and warm.

Last week I came downstairs to find Mum feeding her fresh cream and sardines for breakfast, which isn't so bad for a dustbin kitty. She's kind of irresistible, Krusty. She purrs and pushes against you, and looks at you with those big dark eyes, and that's that – you're in love, like it or not.

A whole lot of stuff has changed around Kirklaggan since Paul left. The high school has a brand-new anti-bullying policy. McKenzie wasn't so bad in the end, once he realized what had been happening right under his nose. Kit and Murphy and Fergus and Tom were excluded from school for a week for bullying, which shocked everyone. As McKenzie always said, they were supposed to be bright, popular lads, a credit to the school. Nobody expected they could be bullies too.

Mum and Dad were horrified, and grounded Kit for a month, but he just shrugged and took it on the chin; I guess he thought he deserved it. He wrote a letter to Paul, saying sorry for his part in the bullying, but Paul never wrote back. Kit said he didn't expect to be forgiven, but that he was sorry all the same, and I believe him.

Anyhow, McKenzie came up with this new scheme where you have trained pupil counsellors who can sort out bullying problems before they get out of hand. Kit, Joey and I all trained, and so did a bunch of other kids, and it seems to be working pretty well so far. We have safe rooms too, like the art room, and specially designated teachers, like Miss Quinn, who can help when stuff gets too complicated for us to sort. I think Paul would have found it a whole lot easier to speak out, the way things are now. I hope so.

Kit is kind of a reformed character these days, but he didn't get back together with Joey. He started dating Karen McKay instead – scary, huh? Still, as Joey said, she's the one who has to stand on the sidelines at footy practice in the pouring rain with her mascara running, her carefully tonged hair getting tangled in the wind and her cream suede kitten-heel boots sinking into the mud. Shame.

Joey reckons she's through with boys, anyhow. She's going to concentrate on her career from now on. Surprise, surprise, she came top of our year in just about every end-of-term exam. What with her part in the anti-bullying policy too, she ended up getting a special award for Pupil of the Year.

There would have been a prize for Paul too – his painting of Krusty and me won the regional final of that art competition. When the picture came back Miss Quinn had it framed and hung it in the school foyer. Ouch. I didn't want to be invisible, but, hey, be careful what you wish for – I didn't want to be quite that *visible*, either.

Paul wasn't around to collect his prize, obviously, but Joey had to go up on stage on the last day of term so McKenzie could present her with the Pupil of the Year plaque. She wore black hipster bootlegs with a black crocheted poncho over the top as a skirt, a black-and-red tie-dyed vest top that she claimed was her PE T-shirt, and red fishnet fingerless gloves. Her stripy hair was backcombed into a huge, fluffy ponytail, with a school tie wrapped round it like a ribbon. Cool.

McKenzie made another announcement that day – we are now, officially, a non-uniform school. McKenzie said he was tired of fighting a losing battle, and that if we chose to look like a tribe of wild Pictish warriors that was our problem, not his.

Jed and Eva thought he felt bad about giving Paul a hard time over the green hair, and that he finally realized that individuality was not a crime against humanity. I think he just realized he'd never outwit Joey Donovan, so he changed tactic and stopped trying.

Was Joey pleased? Well, not so's you'd notice. She reckons half the fun of school was working out ways to bug McKenzie, and that's all over now. She thinks he scrapped the uniform code just to spite her.

There's no pleasing some people, is there?

I sit on the dunes behind Beachcomber Cottage, looking out across the ocean, sipping Cherryade. Seal Island is a moss-green rock, half shadowed and dramatic in the evening sun, lapped by water so blue it looks like wet paint. The tide is going out, and the damp sand is dull and hard-packed, ridged from the waves like the ribcage of a giant from times long gone.

Down by the tideline, there are a couple of beach-magic offerings, stars and circles of shells and seaglass with feathers and twigs and fronds of seaweed spiralling out across the sand. It's not that I believe in beach magic these days – not really. It's just that I know Paul would have liked it this way.

To my right, someone has gathered a whole pile of driftwood sticks, heaped up like a bonfire and ringed with big rocks. Bits and pieces of driftwood that nobody wants, bits that can't be rescued and turned into something useful, something beautiful, something new – they may as well burn as go back to the sea.

The driftwood's me, Paul said once, and I remember wondering how anyone could feel so lost, so lonely, so far out to sea.

Sometimes, I try to imagine a driftwood branch, torn from its tree, its roots, in a storm. I imagine it drifting out on the tide, where the wind and the rain and the salt and the water bleach away the colour, smooth away the roughness. The driftwood branch washes up on a beach, along with a dozen other driftwood branches, with seaweed, tangled string, plastic cartons, old shoes and dead jellyfish. Will somebody pick it up, see its beauty, turn it into something new? Or will they just walk on by, leaving the branch for the tide to take again?

I can't go near the beach, these days, without rescuing at least one piece of driftwood.

I take a long gulp of Cherryade and drain the bottle, shaking out the last few drops beside me. For a moment, they lie there like little specks of blood, and then they sink into the damp sand and fade away before my eyes. I pick up a white gull feather, flecked with brown, and push it into the empty bottle. I drop in some tiny shells, a nugget of green seaglass, a small white pebble mottled with pink like coral. I add a pinch of sand, a sprig of seaweed, and then I kick off my shoes and walk down to the water's edge to scoop up a few drops of ocean.

Paul always reckoned that a message in a bottle needed a letter, a note, but I think that wishes are purer, stronger, when you don't write them down. I blow a little puff of breath into the Cherryade bottle and screw on the lid tightly. Then I wade out into the icy surf and close my eyes and fling the bottle as far as I can. The tide will take it out beyond Seal Island, far out to sea and to the land beyond the sea.

I watch the bottle bob and dip on the waves until it's no more than a glint of light in the distance, and then I turn.

Far away, up on the sand dunes, a lone figure is standing. He walks towards me, his frayed jeans trailing on the sand, his baggy jumper rippling in the breeze. His hair is the colour of toffee, and although I'm still too far away to see, I know that his eyes are blue-green, the colour of the ocean.

'Paul!'

We run towards each other and collide in a muddle of hugs and whoops and squeals, because I never really believed it would happen, not for sure, not till this very moment. But it's happening.

Jed and Eva never gave up. They kept on with the appeals until the social workers finally listened, and because it was what Paul wanted too they took it seriously. It took a while to get the paperwork sorted, but Jed and Eva made sure it happened. They are experts with driftwood, after all.

Paul will have to see a counsellor, and he'll be home-schooled, to start with at least, but he's here. He's home.

Jed and Eva and Mikey and Joey are on the beach now, waving, laughing, shouting down to us. They light the bonfire, and a long pall of smoke drifts down across the beach as the flames take hold. Eva spreads a blanket on the sand, unpacking a big basket of goodies. She threads marshmallows on to long kebab sticks while Joey fusses about, tucking her CD player into a hollow in the dunes and switching the volume up to max. Mikey kicks about at the high-tide line, hunting for something to play football with.

'Party time,' says Paul, resting an arm across my shoulder lazily, the way only best mates can.

'Your hair's different!' I exclaim as we mooch up to the bonfire. 'It's not green any more!'

'Lots of things are different,' he grins, and I see that his eyes are shining, not shadowed, and the sadness he carried around with him like an invisible cloud has faded.

Paul's fingers trace the shape of my cheek softly, like velvet, and I can't work out if that's something friends do too. Maybe just friends like Paul? I get brave, reaching up to stroke the toffee-coloured waves back from his face. He's kept the plaits, skinny ones, braided in with some kind of frayed blue material. Tiny, whorled seashells are stitched in here and there along each plait, and two perfect gull feathers dangle from one, American Indian style. Beach magic.

Maybe it works after all.

Follow your dreams with all cathy cassidy's gorgeous books

Beat Bullying

Almost everyone has been bullied – or bullied others – at some time in their lives. Anyone can be a victim of bullying. It's not your fault, and you don't have to put up with it.
So what can *you* do?

Sometimes, a jokey, clever come-back can defuse the situation. Get people laughing *with* you, not *at* you.

Blank the bullies and walk away from their comments. It's hard to hassle someone who refuses to stand still and be baited.

Don't react. The bully is looking for a weak point, something that really winds you up. No matter how hurt or angry you're feeling, stay cool; it's no fun to pick on someone who won't react.

Don't fight back. It might make things worse – and you could end up in more trouble than the bully.

 Stick with your friends, or if that's not possible, at least avoid being on your own when the bullies are around. Staying near other people makes you less vulnerable.

 Pretend to be confident, even if you're not. Stand tall, pull your shoulders back and try to look confident rather than scared. Practise speaking calmly and clearly. It may be an act, but it really can help – if the bully thinks you are confident, often he/she will leave you alone.

 Write a diary recording each incident of bullying and how it makes you feel – this will help you to explain what's going on if you decide to ask for adult help. It's also a safe way to let out the hurt and anger.

Bullies often warn you not to tell anyone what's happening. Keeping quiet allows them to go on harassing you, so find the courage to speak out. Like Paul in *Driftwood*, it's easy to convince yourself that you can't ask for help – but often, it's the only way to get things sorted.

Confide in your parents, a trusted teacher, a year head, playground supervisor, guidance tutor, school nurse or any adult who will listen, understand and help. Go on speaking out until you get the support you need.

Call a helpline for more advice and back-up, or gather information by surfing an anti-bullying website like those listed here.

Learn to be your own best friend. Bullying can wreck your confidence, so it's important not to let the taunts get under your skin. Believe in yourself, and keep a positive attitude. Don't put yourself down!

FUrther info

What if you're the bully? There are all kinds of reasons why people pick on others, but you *can* change your behaviour. The organizations below can help bullies as well as those being bullied. Don't be afraid to ask for help.

Helplines:

Kidscape: 08451 205 204
Kidscape,
2 Grosvenor Gardens,
London SW1W ODH

ChildLine: 0800 1111
ChildLine, Freepost 1111,
London E1 6GL

websites:

www.**bullywatch.org**

http://**news.bbc.co.uk**/
cbbcnews/hi/static/guides/
bullying/bullying.stm

http://**www.bbc.co.uk**/radio1/
onelife/personal/bullying/
bullying_facts.shtml#help

Books:

Bullying by Michele Elliott

Self-Esteem by Anita Naik

🌸 FRIENDS

try our fun quiz to see

1.

Your best friend seems suddenly moody and troubled. Do you:

a. Ask her quietly what's wrong.

b. Ignore her mood – you're no good with doom and gloom.

c. Plan a special treat to cheer her up.

d. Tell her about beach magic, and show her how to throw her troubles out to sea.

e. Play her your fave goth-chick CD at full blast – it's bound to cheer her up!

2.

Your mate can't stop talking about her latest crush. Do you:

a. Let her talk – it's a bit boring, but you don't really mind.

b. Flirt with him yourself, just for a laugh.

c. Try to fix them up.

d. Draw her a cute cartoon of the two of them together.

e. Tell her about your crush instead – much more interesting!

forever?

how you rate as a mate

3.

One of your friends has big problems at home. Do you:

a. Encourage her to tell a teacher or call a helpline.

b. Steer clear of the subject and focus on doing fun stuff instead.

c. Get her to confide in you and try to work out a solution.

d. Go down to the beach at sunset and write her troubles in the sand for the tide to wash away.

e. Let her know you're there for her, but try not to interfere – she'll sort it when she's ready.

4.

Your mate's been picked for the school play – and you haven't! Do you:

a. Give her a hug to show her how pleased you are for her.

b. Sulk – you'd have been much better.

c. Feel envious, but hide it and help her learn her lines.

d. Feel proud of her – you hate the limelight, but she'll be fab.

e. Write it off to experience – and start auditions for a school band, with you as lead singer!

continues over |||||➡

cathycassidy.com

Friends Forever?

IIII▶ continued

5.

There's a new girl at school who tries to chum up with you and your mates. Do you:

a. Make her feel welcome – it must be awful to have no friends.

b. Make her your new best friend.

c. Take things slowly until you get to know her better.

d. Play it cool – you're not good at making new mates, and you don't want to get hurt.

e. Be friendly – it may last, it may not, but what do you have to lose?

6.

You've rowed with your best friend and fallen out. Do you:

a. Keep your head down and hope it all blows over.

b. Find yourself some new friends – she'll be sorry.

c. Try to patch things up, whether it was your fault or not.

d. Blame yourself – steer clear of her for a while and hope that a bit of beach magic can sort it all out.

e. Forget the fight after five minutes and give her a hug to make up. Friends don't hold grudges!

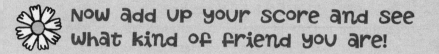

Now add up your score and see what kind of friend you are!

Mostly as:

You're kind, caring and thoughtful, just like **Aisha** in *Indigo Blue*, **Finn** in *Dizzy* and **Hannah** in *Driftwood*. You're a good listener and friends often tell you their troubles – you're one of life's unofficial agony aunts/uncles, and a really brilliant mate.

Mostly bs:

You're a bit too self-centred to be really good mate – like **Jo** in *Indigo Blue*, you can be moody and hate it when others steal the limelight. Get your act together before your friends get fed up and move on...

Mostly cs:

Like **Dizzy**, and **Indie** in *Indigo Blue*, you're a good friend – most of the time! You can be insecure and you don't always know the best way to handle a problem, but you're a fun, loyal friend all the same.

Mostly ds:

Like **Paul** in *Driftwood*, you take time to build a close friendship but once you do, you're a loyal mate with a quirky, offbeat way of solving problems! Boost your self-esteem and learn to trust others a little more and you'll have even more friends.

Mostly es:

You're bright, lively and do things your own way – friendship included! Like **Joey** in *Driftwood*, you're a true friend and fun to have around, though not always as sensitive as you could be when a mate's in trouble. Remember that good friends take time to listen too!

Hiya . . .

One of the coolest things about being a published author is getting the chance to meet my readers! Forget the flash car, the only thing I really wanted to buy with my advance was a VW camper van! It's fab to take it to bookshops, libraries, schools and festivals, and that's how the Cathy Cassidy Friendship Festival evolved. A friendship festival is all about having fun – and making new friends! There's always plenty to do – quizzes, hair-braiding, friendship bracelets, face-painting . . . and music and munchies, of course!

Friendship is something worth celebrating, so why not use these ideas to put on your own Friendship Festival . . . go for it!

Cathy Cassidy
x

Getting ready:

- Send all your friends an invitation telling them where and when the Friendship Festival is happening

- You could ask everyone to dress up for the event and maybe award a prize for the best outfit

cathycassidy.com

On the day:

- Set the scene by decorating the venue with brightly coloured streamers and balloons

- Announce the start of the Friendship Festival and explain how Cathy tours the country with her van

- Gather everyone together and read a chapter from one of Cathy's books

- Friendship bracelets are great fun to make. All you need to do is buy some brightly coloured thread and then plait three strings together. It's easier if you work in pairs and get a bit of adult help to start you off

- There are lots of other things you can do to make your Friendship Festival really special, such as hair-braiding, funky music, make-overs, hand-/face-painting, nail art, T-shirt customizing, drinks and munchies, competitions, sleepovers, henna tattoos and lots of other craft activities (e.g. making bookmarks out of thread and beads). Have fun!

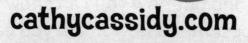

cathycassidy.com

BEST FRIENDS are there for you in the good times and the bad. They can keep a secret and understand the healing power of chocolate.

BEST FRIENDS make you laugh and make you happy. They are there when things go wrong, and never expect any thanks.

BEST FRIENDS are forever,
BEST FRIENDS ROCK!

cathy cassidy's
My Best Friend Rocks!
enter at
cathycassidy.com
mizz
award

IS YOUR BEST FRIEND ONE IN A MILLION?
Go to **cathycassidy.com**
to find out how you can show your
best friend how much you care